GOOD 2 GO

TIED TO A BOSS 3

A Novel

J. L. Rose

Good 2 Go Publishing

TIED TO A BOSS 3
Written by J. L Rose
Cover design: Davida Baldwin
Typesetting: Mychea
ISBN: 9781943686681

Copyright ©2016 Good2Go Publishing
Published 2016 by Good2Go Publishing
7311 W. Glass Lane • Laveen, AZ 85339
www.good2gopublishing.com
https://twitter.com/good2gobooks
G2G@good2gopublishing.com
www.facebook.com/good2gopublishing
www.instagram.com/good2gopublishing

Printed in the USA

TIED TO A BOSS 3

A Novel

J. L. Rose

ACKNOWLEDGEMENTS

First I would like to start this by thanking my heavenly father for this great blessing I've been given. To my family that stood with me and continues to support me no matter my mistakes, I thank you and love you.

To my new family, the entire Good2go Publishing for taking a chance and believing in me. I promise I won't stop until I get us some best sellers. To my uncle William "Peanut" Rose. I'm happy to see you still holding me down play boy. I love you man. To my mom (Mrs. Ludie Rose) and to my father (Mr John L. Rose Senior) I Love the two of you next to god who is number one in my life which makes you number two. But lastly I would like to thank my Fan's and there support and love. I promise to get better and give you all the best of me. Just stay tuned....

Peace and Love

DEDICATION

This book is dedicated to my grandmother's Rosa Mae Rose, Gloria Anderson. I miss and love you both. Rest in peace with the lord.

Prologue

Ignoring the stares, he was receiving as he followed the escorting correctional officer through the hallways at the county jail, Dante headed to the visitation room. He thought about the conversation he just had with his three attorneys who had visited him twenty minutes earlier to discuss his case.

Stopping behind the escorting officer as he stopped in front of a green-painted steel door that read "Visitation" on the front, Dante noticed more officers appearing inside the hallways, all staring at him.

"You've got thirty minutes, Blackwell!" the officer told Dante as he opened the visitation door. He then stepped out of the way, allowing Dante entry.

Not even bothering with responding to the "toy cop" as he walked inside the visitation room, Dante ignored the inmates who were already seated in front of visit windows. Instead, he was now looking for the window at which his visit was supposed to be held.

Showing a small smirk-like smile once he saw Alinna, Dante sat down on the opposite side of one of the visitation glass windows. Seeing the smile, she gave back at him, Dante sat down on the counter instead of the stool in front of the window. He then picked up the phone just as Alinna picked up the phone on her side.

"Hey, baby . . . You okay?" Alinna asked as she sat staring Dante over, wishing she could hug him.

"Where's James?" Dante asked, ignoring Alinna's question about his well-being.

Shaking her head and smiling up at Dante, Alinna lowered the phone from her ear and looked to her right, where James stood a few feet away. Catching James's eyes, Dante nodded him over.

Seeing James as he walked up beside Alinna, Dante felt himself relax at the sight of his boy, nodding his head to the white boy before shifting his eyes back to a smiling Alinna.

"You feel better now?" Alinna asked, still smiling up at Dante.

"I'm good!" he answered before adding, "I just had a visit from the lawyer, Jonathan King, and two other lawyers who were with him. So far, shit's looking just as I figured it would, and I don't have a bond."

"I spoke with Jonathan also," Alinna told him. "I also got the two other attorneys for you. I figure they could help out Jonathan with this case."

Nodding his head, Dante then said, "I've been thinking about all of this shit with how everything played out, and something not right."

"What do you mean?" Alinna asked, staring hard at Dante.

"I'm not really sure yet," Dante told Alinna, playing a few things around in his mind. "How was Monica and those MDPD cops able to put us in all of this together? Something don't seem right."

"Alex . . . Dante!" Alinna told him. "He was undercover, remember?"

"Naw . . . !" Dante said, shaking his head. "It's something else, Alinna. I'ma figure it out, but I'ma need you to make sure everything on point out there, alright?"

"What else was you expecting me to do?" Alinna told Dante, staring into his eyes while noticing the expression he got when he was plotting or planning something.

1

A linna walked through the parking lot of the county jail after visiting with Dante. She hated seeing him locked up, even though he didn't seem bothered about it. Alinna nodded to her armed personal chauffeur who Dante had handpicked. She then climbed into the back of her new Rolls Royce Phantom she received from Dante for her birthday on the same night that he had turned himself in to keep her from being locked up.

Hearing James talking with the driver as she slid across the backseat of the Phantom, Alinna sat next to the window, staring outside as she easily formed a picture of Dante in her mind.

"Alinna, you alright?" James asked as he climbed into the Phantom and noted the expression on her face.

"We gotta get him outta there, James," she told her personal bodyguard and close friend who Dante had brought into the family. "I hate seeing him down here in this place."

"What did he say about the lawyers?" James asked. "Did he mention them coming to see him yet?"

"They've met up with Dante. But he says that there's no bond right now but they're fighting to get him one," she explained. She then changed the conversation. "Dante told me something, James. He said that something wasn't right with how the case went down."

"What about that Alex Whitehead dude?" James asked, cutting in on what Alinna was saying.

"I mentioned that to Dante," Alinna said as she slowly shook her head while looking over at James. "He said it's not just Alex. He thinks it's bigger than Alex, but he's not sure what yet."

"What do you think?" James asked, just as his cell phone went off inside of his pocket.

Turning her attention back out the window, not bothering with answering James's question even though she was already mentally playing back things in her head, Alinna lost her train of thought as her cell phone went off from inside her Chanel bag.

Digging out her iPhone, she caught James mentioning one of his security men's names, since James was placed to oversee security by her and Dante.

Alinna looked at the phone screen and saw that it was Vanessa. "Yeah, Vanessa . . . what's up?"

"Where you at?" Vanessa asked, yelling over the music that was playing in the background.

"Nessa, turn down the fucking music!" Alinna yelled into the phone, hearing the music lowered a few moments later.

"Sorry, girl!" Vanessa apologized. "That's Andre's ass with all that damn Jay-Z shit. Where you at, though?"

"We just left from seeing Dante. Why?"

"How my brother doing?"

"Dante still Dante. What up though?"

"We riding over to meet up with Harmony and Amber over in Brown Sub. They want us to meet them out in the new spot Harmony just opened up. It's these two new workers they want you to meet out there."

Shifting her eyes over to James, Alinna said into the phone, "It'll have to be later on, Nessa. I gotta take care of something for Dante. Then I need to handle something myself."

After talking with Vanessa a few more minutes, Alinna hung up. Looking back over toward James, she asked, "What's up, James?"

"Jose and Javier just checked in," James told her. "The new connect, Goldmen, is headed to the hotel with Jose and Javier now."

"What about Mr. Sutter?" Alinna asked, concerned about the arrival of the new cocaine connect that Dante had set up to meet with the family.

"He hasn't arrived yet!" James told her. He then explained, "I've already sent a message to his personal assistant asking when we can expect his arrival. They're on their way now."

Nodding her head in response, Alinna turned her focus back out her window, allowing her mind to wander back to what she and Dante had discussed over visitation.

* * *

Making it back to the jail unit almost twenty minutes after his visitation ended with Alinna and James, Dante started straight toward the phone area as soon as he entered the unit. Walking past the officer's desk that was stationed at the front of the open bay jail unit, near the door, Dante ignored the stare he was receiving from the female officer seated behind the desk.

Stopping in front of the last phone at the end of the row of five, in the corner, Dante picked up the headset and went about punching in a phone number. But he shifted his eyes to his right as he noticed two inmates walking past a few feet away, staring straight at him.

3

Hearing someone answer the line and accept the call a few moments later, Dante turned his back and faced the wall so he could face out overlooking the unit.

"Hello!"

"Yeah. What's up, Angela?"

"Oh my God, Dante! Baby, I've been so worried about you. I've been checking on things with how your case is going and—"

"Angela . . . relax!" Dante told her, cutting her off as she ran off at the mouth. "I don't wanna talk about the case over the phone. I want you to come down here to see me. I wanna talk to you about something."

"Dante, I don't know if I can. You know what position I'm in, and if it gets tied in that—"

"Don't worry about that!" Dante said, cutting Angela off again. "You'll get a visit soon, and everything will be explained then. What's up with my daughter?"

"She's been asking about you."

"Tell her I said I love her and I'll see her soon."

"I'll tell her. Are you doing okay, though?"

"Yeah, I'm good," Dante answered as he watched the same two inmates out of the corner of his eye, standing at the opening that led inside of the bathroom area.

Continuing his phone call with Angela until the phone call ended, Dante hung up the phone and then stared across the unit toward his bed area. Out of the corner of his eyes, he saw that the two inmates were still staring at him from the bathroom area.

"Blackwell!" he heard his name being called as he passed the officer's desk.

He stopped and turned his head to look at the female officer and asked, "What's the problem, Officer?"

"Ain't no problem. I just wanted to talk to you for a second," she told Dante, smiling at him. "You don't remember me, do you?"

Staring a moment and somewhat recognizing the face, Dante opened his mouth to admit he didn't know the pretty, brown-skinned female, when it finally came to him. "Yeah! I remember you from some time back. You a CO, huh?"

"Mmmm-huh . . . ," she answered, still smiling. "I've been here almost five years, but shit happens, and I'm still a CO. I never thought I would see you here, though, even though you do your thing out there."

"I ain't super—"

"Ms. Cook . . . ," Dante was interrupted, looking to his left to see one of the two inmates who was watching him.

"I know yo ass see me talking," she told the inmate, with an attitude. "You better go find yourself something to do and learn some respect."

Dante saw the look on the homeboy's face but caught the way he shot him a look before walking off. Dante slowly shook his head as he looked back at the female officer as she said, "I'm sorry, Blackwell. These niggas in here don't got no respect."

Smirking at how the female officer's attitude reminded him a little of Alinna, Dante asked, "What's your name again, shorty?"

"Call me Kerri," she told Dante, smiling again.

"Alright, Kerri. Call me Dante," he told her as his mind was already at work, putting together a plan inside of his head.

*   *   *

Alinna met up with Mr. Goldmen, the new heroin connect that Dante set up to go into business with the family, as well as with Mr. Sutter, who finally showed up. Alinna sat talking business with both drug lords. Upon mentioning their debt to Dante, she noticed how both men's expressions changed upon hearing his name.

Reaching an agreement and understanding on their business together, Alinna left both men. James followed beside her as they exited out of the hotel and out to the Phantom.

"What do you think, James?" Alinna asked once she and James were inside the backseat of the Phantom.

"Personally . . . ," James began as he looked down at his phone and read a text he just received, "I don't like either of them, but I know they both fear and respect Dante after what he did and gave them."

"What did he give 'em?" Alinna asked, staring at James with a questioning look on her face.

"Their lives!" he told her, answering her question with a small smile.

Shaking her head, unable to help but smile after hearing James's answer and thinking about Dante, Alinna said after a moment, "We need to talk to Angela."

"Is that where we're going now?" James asked, waiting for Alinna's next order.

"In a minute!" she told him as she pulled out her cell phone to make a quick phone call to check on other business.

2

Alinna ignored her personal feelings and met up with Angela at a coffee shop in North Miami Beach to handle something that Dante had asked her to handle. Alinna made the meeting as fast as she could, dropping off a small brown envelope that she had picked up from an associate of the family.

"What's this?" Angela asked with a slight attitude after Alinna simply tossed it onto the table in front of her, before turning to leave.

"It'll get you in to see Dante," Alinna answered, staring back at Angela with her face balled up. "I don't know what he even wanna see you for, though."

Hearing Alinna's parting words before she left, Angela sucked her teeth as she opened up the envelope. As she turned the envelope upside down, an ID fell out onto the table.

Climbing back inside the Phantom as James and the driver stood waiting for her, Alinna got comfortable in her seat as James climbed in beside her.

"That was fast!" James said as the driver shut the car door.

"I can't stand that bitch!" Alinna replied as she pulled out her cell phone and dialed Vanessa's number.

"Yeah . . . Who this?"

"Nessa, where you at?"

"I'm at the penthouse with everybody. Where you at?"

"I'm about to meet up with this real estate agent and look at this new house. I want you to meet me at this address," Alinna told her, giving Vanessa the new address to the house to which they might be moving.

After hanging up with Vanessa and then calling the real estate agent who helped them with their first house, Alinna explained to the agent that she was ready to meet and that she was headed over to the new house.

"James, how many men you have following us?" Alinna asked as soon as she hung up with the agent.

Surprised she even realized they were being followed, James asked, "When did you notice?"

"I noticed earlier after we left the jail, but now it's more than before," Alinna told him before further explaining, "You forgot who my man is, James?"

Smiling at her question, James answered, "Dante was the one who said he wanted a team around you when you're out. There are two Range Rovers with five of our men in each of them."

Alinna shook her head and smiled, picturing Dante demanding James have more of their men around to protect her. She looked out of her window, hating where Dante was at.

They arrived at the new house twenty minutes later, pulling up in front of a tall black gate in Hollywood, Florida. Sitting inside, Alinna stared out of the Phantom's back window at a two-story mansion that was actually bigger than she expected it to be.

Alinna saw the Mercedes pull up beside her and watched as the real estate agent climbed from the Benz and waved to her. The agent walked toward the gate and pressed a few buttons on the security intercom attached to the gate. The agent returned to her car and drove through the now opened gates as the Phantom followed.

Following the Benz up the long drive that turned off in front of the main house and continued around toward the back part of the mansion, the driver parked. James then climbed out from the Phantom and held open the door for Alinna.

"Alinna, it's good to see you again," the real estate agent said with a big smile as she walked up to Alinna and gave her a hug.

"Alinna!" James called, getting Alinna's attention. He nodded his head toward the front gate and said, "There's Vanessa pulling up."

Seeing Dre's Land Rover and Tony T's Aston Martin at the front gate, Alinna looked over to James and said, "Send one of the security to open the gate."

"The code is 26, 19, 20," the real estate agent announced as she smiled over at James.

* * *

"This is a one-of-a-kind masterpiece," the real estate agent told Alinna and the others as she led them into the mansion. She continued, "It has panoramic water views from the sweeping 280-degree lot-and-a-half estate. It has a private 100-foot floating dock, plus an additional lift and watercraft floating pad. Fully gated and fenced, this estate offers privacy and security. There's full-house automation, with video, audio, and a full theater. The unique single-level floor plan features five luxury bedroom suites and a sixth suite designed as a private guest quarters with its own kitchen and private entrance. The master bedroom suite includes his-and-her baths, a morning kitchen, a dramatic shower looking out to the private orchid gardens, and designer closets. The owner's retreat is just off the master bedroom. There is a 1,000-bottle wine room and a full bar, a dramatic pool with reflecting fountains and spa, and a bridge over the koi pond leads to the dock . . ."

They listened to the real estate agent as they all followed her through the house, looking over everything. Alinna watched the family's reaction to the house. Once Amber and Harmony had the agent's attention, Alinna pulled Vanessa to the side and asked, "What you think, Vanessa?"

"You mean about the house?" Vanessa asked, smiling. "Girl, you know I love it!"

"You think Dante gonna like it, Vanessa?"

"Alinna, that's your man!" Vanessa told her playfully. "You know my brother will love anything you pick out, since he crazy about you."

"So, Alinna, what do you think?" the real estate agent asked, smiling as she walked up on Alinna and Vanessa.

"How much are you asking?" Alinna inquired, meeting and holding the agent's eyes.

"The asking price is $12 million," she responded.

"God damn!" James said under his breath from a few feet away after hearing the price.

Cutting her eyes over to a smiling James, Alinna looked back at the agent and asked, "How fast can we move in?"

* * *

Alinna was back at the penthouse that Dante moved everyone into right before he was taken into custody. She was inside the master bedroom, laid across the bed with her son D.J., when the house phone rang next to her head on the bedside table.

She reached over and picked up the cordless phone from its base. Alinna placed the receiver to her ear to hear the collect call operator ask if she would accept the call from a Dante Blackwell from the Miami-Dade County Jail. She accepted the call by pressing 5.

"What's up, shorty?"

10

"Hey, baby," Alinna said, smiling at hearing Dante's voice. "I was wondering when you was going to call me. Everything okay?"

"Everything good on this end. You take care of that thing I asked you to handle?"

"Yes, Dante," Alinna answered, rolling her eyes thinking about Angela. "I gave that to her earlier. But anyway, I went by and saw the new house. You'll like it!"

"How big is it?"

"It has five bedrooms and a sixth bedroom with private guest quarters. It also has a separate retreat away from the main house."

"You like it?"

"Dante, I love it, baby. I already started the process to buy it."

"Yeah, alright. Where my lil' man at?"

"He right here watching TV with me," Alinna replied. "You don't wanna know how much the house is, Dante?"

"Knowing you, I'm pretty sure it's up there. Put my lil' man on the phone."

Alinna smiled as she handed the phone to her son, telling him that his father was on the line. She laid back and watched D.J. talk and laugh with his father. She reached out and ran her hand through his short, curly black hair, smiling as she stared at the spitting image of Dante.

Alinna took the phone back from D.J., placed it up to her ear, and asked, "Yeah, baby?"

"Alinna . . . listen! I've been doing some thinking about what I was telling you about at visitation. Something really don't feel right about all this. I've got something in the works, but I'll explain it to you at the next visit."

"Also, I had that meeting with our new friends you told me to meet with."

"How'd it go?" Dante asked, instantly knowing she was talking about the new connects.

"Everything went perfect once I mentioned your name to them."

"That's good," Dante replied, and then continued, "You got that new shipment from what's his name?"

"I haven't heard anything from him since you came home," Alinna told Dante, understanding he was speaking about Dominic Saldana.

Quiet for a few moments, Dante finally spoke up, "Look, Alinna, this phone about to hang up, but make sure you get out here next week . . . Monday . . . so we can talk. I love you, shorty."

"I love you too, Dante!"

Hearing the phone hang up, Alinna put it down. She then got comfortable in the bed and wished that Dante was lying next to her.

* * *

Unable to sleep the entire plane ride to Miami, since she was overly worried about her child's father, Natalie Saldana looked over to her right as one of her armed security men walked up beside her seat. She smiled when she noticed that it was Gomez, her personal security bodyguard.

"Natalie, we're about to land in three minutes," he told her, taking his seat across from her on her personal jet that her father bought her for her eighteenth birthday.

Natalie could feel how fast her heart was beating. She just wanted to get off the jet and find out in which jail Dante was being held. She all but jumped out of her seat as soon as the plane came to a stop, ignoring Gomez as he called out behind her.

Rushing to the front of the plane as soon as the jet stopped rolling and the engine was shut off, Natalie rushed Gomez to hurry and open the door. She was off the plane within moments of the door being opened and the mobile stairs being placed in front of the door to the jet.

Natalie saw Greg Wilson, who used to work for her father but was now employed by Dante. She rushed over to the middle-aged man as he stood next to a metallic black Maybach Benz, with two Benz trucks parked behind him.

"Ms. Saldana . . . !"

"Where is Dante?" Natalie cut him off as he was about to greet her.

"Okay . . . ," Greg said as he turned to face the Maybach. He laid his briefcase on the top of the hood of the Benz and opened it. He then pulled out a file and handed it to Natalie and said, "This is everything I was able to get on Mr. Blackwell. As of right now, he's down at the Miami-Dade County Jail."

"Gomez . . . that's where we're—"

"Ms. Saldana, you cannot visit Mr. Blackwell at this moment," Greg interrupted before quickly continuing upon seeing the upset expression in her face. "Mr. Blackwell may not have any more visitors until tomorrow morning at 7:00 a.m. Visitation is finished for today."

"Damn it!" Natalie stated, looking down at her rose gold lady Rolex and seeing that it was already after 6:00 p.m. She sighed loudly, looked back at Greg, and asked, "Where have you placed us, Greg Wilson?"

Pulling keys and a small white envelope from his briefcase, he handed over the items to Natalie and explained, "I've leased the whole top floor at the Grand Plaza for you and your security duty, Ms. Saldana."

Thanking Greg and expressing that she would call him the next day, Natalie handed over both keys and an envelope to Gomez and then walked over to the back door of the Maybach while pulling out her cell phone to call her mother.

"Natalie?" Carmen Saldana answered on the other end of the phone.

"Yes, mother!" Natalie answered as she climbed inside the backseat of the Maybach once Gomez unlocked and opened the back door for her. "I'm just landing in Miami now and heading to our hotel."

"What have you found out from Wilson about Dante, Natalie?"

"He's being held at the Miami-Dade County Jail, but I will not be able to see him until tomorrow," Natalie told her. "Greg Wilson also gave me a file on Dante. I'm going to read over what's inside."

"Alright, sweetheart. Let me know if you need anything that can help you get Dante out of that jail."

"I will, Mother," Natalie replied, pausing a few seconds before asking, "What about Daddy? Is he still upset?"

"Sweetheart, you know your father. He will be alright," Carmen told her daughter. "You just focus on what you went to Miami for, which is freeing Dante. Do you understand me, Natalie?"

Nodding her head even though her mother couldn't see her, Natalie answered, "I understand, Mother. I'll call you later."

"Love you, sweety!"

Hanging up with her mother and sliding her cell phone back inside her Dolce & Gabbana bag, Natalie looked toward the front seat at Gomez behind the steering wheel, who asked, "You okay, Natalie?"

"I'm okay, Gomez," Natalie told her friend and bodyguard, meeting his eyes in the rearview mirror. She then gave him the address of the hotel off a sticky note that was inside the file.

"We'll get him out, Natalie," Gomez told her, meeting her eyes once again before he focused back on the road.

*   *   *

Natalie read over the file that Greg Wilson had given her on what was happening with Dante's case and charges. She realized where she was only after Gomez called her name to announce that he was pulling in the Maybach to park at the Grand Plaza Hotel on South Beach in Miami.

She put away the file and then climbed out of the car once her door was opened. Natalie followed behind Gomez while her team of security surrounded her. She noticed all the stares as she entered the lobby of the hotel.

After allowing Gomez to handle everything at the front desk, Natalie then followed him onto the elevator, along with three members of her security team behind. She stood there thinking about the murder of the law enforcement and federal agent personnel along with his many other charges.

Following Gomez off the elevator on the penthouse floor, Natalie stopped behind him as he stopped in front of her suite door. She entered the penthouse once he opened the door. Gomez remained outside in the hall talking with security.

After finding the master bedroom, Natalie tossed her bag onto the bed and sat down on the foot of it. She then went back to reading Dante's file to see what they were up against.

3

Dante heard his name as he was waking up from the light sleep he was in. He opened his eyes and looked at the officer standing at the front of the unit. He sat up in bed to see the male officer waving him over.

Swinging his legs over the left side of the bottom bunk he was in, Dante slid his feet into the jailhouse shoes that Officer Kerri had given him to wear, since his pair of Stacy Adams were taken on the day he turned himself in. He then stood up and walked over toward the officer's desk.

"Blackwell, you've got somebody down at visitation trying to get in to see you," the officer told Dante. "She's not on your visit list. You wanna add her?"

"Who is it?" Dante asked, staring at the officer with a confused look.

"Hold on!" the officer responded as he spoke into the phone and requested the name of the visitor. He looked back toward Dante and announced, "It's Natalie Saldana downstairs. You wanna put her on your list or not?"

"Yeah . . . ," Dante answered, surprised to hear Natalie was at the jail to see him. "Go 'head and put her on."

Dante got himself ready for his visit with Natalie and then followed the escorting officer from the unit once he was picked up. Dante wondered if Dominic was also down in Miami with her.

Once he reached the visitation area, Dante entered the room. After the door shut and locked behind him, he walked past the first three visit booths and then saw Natalie, with Gomez standing behind her. She sat down and smiled at him once she saw him.

"I love you!" Natalie cried as soon as she and Dante picked up the phone receivers. Still smiling, she added, "I miss you so much."

"What are you doing here, Natalie?" Dante asked as he sat down on the counter.

"You don't sound like you miss me, Dante," she told him with a pout, which caused him to smile down on her.

"I miss you too, Natalie," Dante told her before asking, "But what are you doing here?"

"I got here last night after I found out you was locked up."

"Where's Dominic?" he asked, shifting his eyes to Gomez, nodding his head in greeting to the big Spanish bodyguard. After receiving a nod in return, Dante looked back at Natalie to see the change in her expression. "Natalie, what's wrong? What's up with Dominic?"

"Dante . . . Daddy isn't here in Miami with me, and he isn't coming!" she explained, staring straight into Dante's eyes.

Slowly nodding his head in understanding of what Natalie was actually telling him, Dante changed the subject by asking, "You talk to Greg Wilson yet?"

"He met me when we got here," she answered. "Baby, what can we do? I've read up on what you're being charged with. What can we do? Mother said she will help us in any way we need her help."

"That's good to know," Dante replied as ideas began flooding his mind. "I'm actually happy you're here. There's something I've been trying to figure out, and you may help me in figuring all this out. I'll explain."

*   *   *

Hearing her cell phone begin to ring inside her Gucci bag just as she was climbing inside her Phantom, Alinna pulled out the phone as James was climbing into the car beside her.

Smiling at hearing it was a collect call from Dante, Alinna accepted it and said, "Hey baby. You calling me early. What's up?"

"Alinna . . . look! I just had a visit from Natalie. She's here in Mia—"

"Whoa!" Alinna said, cutting off Dante, unsure she was hearing him correctly. "You said you just had a visit from who, Dante? Natalie?"

"Yeah, Alinna," he answered. "Baby, don't trip out. We already talked about this, and now isn't the time to be fighting about this."

"Dante, we talked about this before you went to jail. What the fuck is she doing down here?"

"She's here to help, Alinna."

"Help?" Alinna said, raising her voice. "What the fuck can she do that I can't, Dante?"

Sighing into the phone, Dante calmly said, "That's just it, Alinna. The both of you are going to be working together on something I've been putting together inside my head. Something isn't right, and I need you to do this for me, shorty. You gonna do this for me, or am I fighting alone?"

Sucking her teeth, Alinna asked, "What do you want me to do?"

"That's my shorty!" Dante said, but then added, "Here's Natalie's number. I want you to call her now. I'll call you back this afternoon by 3:00."

"Whatever, Dante!"

"I love you too."

"Mmm-huh!" Alinna replied, hanging up the phone yet unable to keep from smiling after hearing him tell her that he loved her.

Alinna called the number that Dante had given her. She sat and listened to the line ring twice, when a Spanish-accented female voice answered the phone and said, "Hello."

"Is this Natalie?"

"Yes, it is. And I'm guessing this is Alinna."

"Correct," Alinna answered with a slight attitude. "Listen, I'm calling because Dante asked me to call."

"I have instructions from Dante, but I'd rather not talk about them over the phone. Can we meet?"

"Where are you?"

"Where do you want to meet?"

Smirking at the woman's response, Alinna said, "Alright. Meet me at Granny B's Soul Food."

Alinna gave Natalie the address and then hung up. She looked at James, saw him smirking, and asked, "What?"

"You two are completely different but are completely the same when it comes to Dante," James explained, fully smiling now.

"You mean you know her?" Alinna asked, balling up her face as she stared at him.

"I spent time with her and Dante, so I'm pretty sure how you and she will respond to one another."

"I don't like her!" Alinna told him as she turned to look out the window.

"I wonder why!" James said, shaking his head and smiling at Alinna.

* * *

Angela pulled her new Lincoln Continental into the parking lot down at the county jail, parking in the visitation area. She shut off the engine and then grabbed her recently bought Gucci bag. She climbed out of the car, started across the parking lot, and headed toward the front entrance of the jail.

She noticed the long line as soon as she walked into the visitation area of the jail. Angela sighed deeply, as she was really not in the mood to have to stand in line to wait to see Dante. However, she was willing to do it because she wanted to see him and maybe even make him an offer, depending on his response to what she had to ask him.

Pulling out her cell phone while waiting in the slow-moving line, Angela saw the three numbers with blocked-out names on her phone. She was certain they were from Dante, since he was probably wondering where she was because she had arrived later than the time she told him she'd be there.

Finally making it to the front desk, Angela stepped up to a young, dark-skinned female officer and asked, "I'm here to visit with Dante Blackwell. He has visits today, right?"

"And you are?" the female officer asked while looking Angela over with an attitude.

"I'm Lisa Hernandez," Angela told her, ignoring the way she was being looked at and while digging out the fake ID that Alinna had given her the day before to visit him.

The officer took the ID from Angela and then punched a few keys into the computer's keyboard. She then looked back to Angela and said, "Ummm . . . Ms. Hernandez, Mr. Blackwell has already had both of his visits for the week."

"Excuse me?" Angela asked, not believing what she just heard. "You must be mistaken, ma'am. Dante Blackwell couldn't have had both his visits yet. He's expect—"

"Ma'am, I'm sorry," the female officer said, cutting off Angela as she handed her back her fake ID. "Mr. Blackwell will have another chance at visitation come Monday of next week. You may come back then."

"Can you tell me who it was who visited with him, please?" Angela asked as the officer handed her back the ID.

"I'm sorry, ma'am," the officer responded. "We cannot give out that information. I'm sorry again."

Sucking her teeth as she turned away from the front desk and ignoring the smirk on the female officer's face, Angela stormed from the jail, cursing in Spanish as she headed toward her car. She couldn't believe that Dante had her drive all the way out to the jail to visit him, only to be turned away.

Angela unlocked and snatched open the door to her car as she angrily dropped into the driver's seat and felt tears run down her face. She found herself grow even angrier for crying over Dante, after everything she had to put up with for him.

"Let me find out some bitch . . . ," Angela started as she snatched her phone from her bag and then punched in a few numbers.

"Miami-Dade County Jail," a male voice answered after two rings.

"Hello . . . this is Captain Angela Perez with the Miami-Dade Police Department. Can you put me through to whoever it is that's over visitation, please?"

"Hold please," a male voice said, clicking over the line, only for a female's voice to come over the line and ask, "Hello. Visitation Department. This is Sergeant Lee. How can I help you?"

Introducing herself again, just as she had done with the male voice that answered the first time, Angela then said, "I'm looking for some information on one of your inmates."

"His or her name, Captain Perez."

"Dante Blackwell."

"Okay, Captain Perez. I have information right in front of me. What can I help you with, ma'am?"

"Can you look and tell me everyone who is on Mr. Blackwell's visitation list, please?"

"There are four names here, ma'am."

"Okay. Can you just tell me the two visits that Mr. Blackwell had this week?"

"Hold please," the woman responded. She then continued, "Mr. Blackwell received a visit from a Ms. Alinna Rodriguez yesterday, and today there was a visit from a Ms. Natalie Saldana."

"What did you say that name was again?" Angela asked, wanting to hear the name one more time.

"It's Natalie Saldana, Captain Perez."

"Thank you very much," Angela replied, hanging up the phone.

*　*　*

The Maybach Benz pulled inside the parking lot at Granny B's Soul Food, followed by two Benz trucks. Alinna continued eating her lunch of rib tips, yellow rice, collard greens, sweet cornbread, and candied yams while James sat across from her enjoying his fried chicken wings, macaroni and cheese, and a few other sides.

"They're here!" Alinna spoke up right before taking a drinking from her fruit punch.

"I know," James replied as he continued eating his food.

Alinna smiled a small grin as she stared over at James. She shook her head and looked back out the window just in time to see the back door being opened by a tall, muscular, Spanish man dressed in a suit. She then shifted her eyes to the slim, light-skinned woman who climbed out of the Maybach. She was dressed in a full-length dress that hugged her body perfectly and showed off her nice, curvy build.

"That's Natalie there!" James said, also staring at her out the window. He then turned and looked at one of his security personnel and nodded to him to go and greet Natalie.

"That her boyfriend with her?" Alinna asked as she continued watching Natalie and the big man with whom she was walking and talking.

"That's Gomez!" James replied. "Yeah, he's Natalie's personal bodyguard and friend."

Not even bothering to count how many men Natalie had for security, yet seeing more than ten surrounding her, Alinna went back to eating as James stood up when Natalie and Gomez were escorted over to their table.

"James!" Natalie said, smiling as she and James embraced each other. "It's good to see you."

"You look good, Natalie," James replied, smiling at her. He then nodded at Gomez before finally introducing Alinna: "Natalie, this is Alinna Rodriguez."

"So you're the Alinna I've heard so much about!" Natalie said as Alinna slowly stood up from her seat and ran her eyes over the other woman, admitting to herself that Dante's son's mother was extremely beautiful.

"Dante's told me about you as well," Alinna said as she held out her hand to Natalie.

"We'll let you two talk," James suggested as he and Gomez turned and started to walk over to the next table across from the women.

Alinna motioned for Natalie to have a seat as she herself sat back down. She then nodded her thanks to James as he cleared the table, taking his and her trays. She then looked back toward Natalie and asked, "So tell me. How far along are you with this pregnancy?"

"A few weeks," Natalie answered before adding, "and, yes, I'm sure Dante is the father of our baby."

"Relax!" Alinna told her, showing a small smile. "I believe Dante if he says it's his baby, so that's why I didn't outright question you."

Nodding her head in response, Natalie sighed softly and then said, "Alinna . . . look. I understand you don't like the fact that I'm a part of Dante's life. Just like I don't like that he still loves you after everything you two have been through. But I love Dante, and whatever it takes to make him happy is what I'm willing to do."

"Then I guess we both agree on something then," Alinna told her while slowly smiling, just as Natalie began to smile back. "So what is it that Dante is plotting now?"

Leaning forward toward Alinna, Natalie told her in a lowered voice what Dante was planning and what he wanted them to do.

4

Dante watched the news that was playing on the unit's TV as he lay half asleep on his bunk. He looked over toward the phone area and saw a phone finally open up next to an inmate that had spent the last twenty minutes making calls. Dante left his bunk and started toward the phones. He passed the officer's desk where Officer Jefferson sat mean-mugging him, with a balled-up face.

Ignoring the officer, Dante continued walking over toward the phones. He stopped in front of the last phone next to the wall. Just as he was about to grab the headset, another inmate snatched up the receiver before he could.

"I'm next . . . right here," the inmate told Dante, smirking sarcastically at him.

Dante recognized him as one of the same two inmates who before had been shooting him looks and trying to get in his way. Dante leaned slightly forward and looked past the inmate. He then nodded his head and asked, "You see that?"

Moving just as soon as the inmate barely turned his head to look to his right, Dante slammed an open hand and turned sideways, hitting the inmate in the throat. This caused the inmate to drop the phone receiver as Dante grabbed his throat. Dante caught the phone receiver and then gently reached out with his free right hand and pushed the gasping-for-breath inmate away. He dialed Angela's phone number.

Hearing Angela finally answer the phone, Dante sat waiting until she accepted the collect call, and never got a chance to speak, as Angela went off yelling.

"You lying, game-playing bastard! Who the hell is Natalie Saldana?" Angela yelled into the phone. Before he could answer, she continued, "I drove way out there to visit your ass and waited in a long line for over twenty minutes, only to be told you had a visit from that bitch Alinna and some bitch named Natalie Saldana. Who the fuck is she, Dante?"

"You finished yet?" Dante asked once Angela finally shut up.

"Nigga, don't play with me!" Angela told him, spitting her words at Dante.

Ignoring Angela's attitude, Dante said, "First, I tried to call you to tell you not to drive . . ."

"Muthafucker, you need to . . . !"

"Angela, shut the fuck up!" Dante demanded in a quiet voice, which caused Angela to stop talking. He continued, "I called you to tell you not to drive out here, but you never answered your phone. And to answer your question about Natalie, she's someone I met while I was out of town."

"Why is she here, and why did you accept a visit from her when you knew I was coming?"

"Angela . . . look!"

"Answer the damn question, Dante!"

"She's my baby's mother, and she wanted to see me, alright?" Dante replied, giving Angela what she wanted. He was tired of her asking about Natalie.

Angela remained quiet for a full minute, unable to believe what she just heard Dante admit to her. She finally got control of herself and asked, "Dante, what the hell do you mean she's your baby's mother? Matter of fact, nigga, fuck you! I don't even want to hear shit else you got to say. I was gonna offer you a way out of this mess you're in, but I can care less what the fuck happens to you. Fuck you, nigga! I hope it was worth turning yourself in for that bitch Alinna."

Hearing Angela hang up the phone in his face, Dante stood where he was for a moment but finally hung up.

Leaving the phone area and playing back the conversation in his head that he just had with Angela, Dante felt that something was not right. But he was unable to pinpoint exactly what was said that was bugging him. Dante stepped into the shower/restroom area and walked up to the second sink, with the good mirror.

He turned on the cold water and splashed his face a few times. Dante then sat up from the sink, wiping his face, when he caught movement from his left-hand side. He looked to his left to see homeboy from out by the phone standing there along with two more inmates that were with him.

Dante smirked and let out a light laugh as he turned to face the three inmates. He locked eyes with the inmate from the phone area. As Dante nodded, the inmate rushed him.

Just as the inmate swung at him, Dante caught his forearm and then stepped into him, kicking out one of his legs and tripping him. He then followed through with a solid forearm to homeboy's face that sent blood flying and the guy slamming down to the ground hard.

He shifted his eyes to the other two inmates, who both took steps backward. Dante shook his head as he turned back to the sink, washed his hands and forearm, left the shower/restroom, and walked right past both inmates.

Dante noticed the surprised look on Officer Jefferson's face as he was walking past his desk. Dante made it a point to meet the officer's eyes as he continued walking back to his bunk. He was pretty certain that Officer Jefferson was responsible for his visit from the three inmates.

* * *

Listening to the phone ringing as she called Dante's attorney, Jonathan King, Alinna sat in the backseat with James as they road in her Phantom. After leaving Granny B's, she replayed her conversation with Natalie about what Dante was putting together while still locked up. When she heard the attorney answer his phone, Alinna said, "Mr. King, this is Alinna Rodriguez. Do you have a moment?"

"Hello, Mrs. Blackwell. What can I do for you today?"

Smiling at the title the attorney gave her, Alinna said, "Mr. King, I've spoken with Dante, and he's asked me to speak with you about a few things concerning the case. Can you meet me at the penthouse and bring what information you have on everyone that's on Dante's case?"

"How is tonight at 7:00, Mrs. Blackwell?"

"I'll see you at 7:00, Mr. King," Alinna told the attorney.

"Everything alright, Alinna?" James asked as soon as she hung up the phone.

Nodding her head in response, Alinna turned her head and stared out the window as she began wondering exactly what Dante was really up to.

Alinna lost her train of thought once the Phantom came to a stop and James spoke up announcing that they were at their destination. She then turned her head and looked out the opposite window at the two-story royal blue and white house that was in a middle-class neighborhood.

Climbing from the Phantom once James opened the door for her, Alinna stepped from the car and received a nod from her driver. When she heard her name, she looked toward the right to see both Vanessa and Harmony walking toward her. She saw Vanessa's truck that was parked in of the driveway to the house.

"You finally decided to make your way around this way, huh?" Vanessa said, rolling her eyes at Alinna as she and Harmony stopped in front of Alinna. "Hey, James! What's up?"

"What up, Vanessa?" James replied while looking around the area, since Alinna had dismissed the security, leaving only James and the armed driver.

"How my boo doing, Alinna?" Harmony asked with a smile.

"Harmony, you know how Dante is," Alinna told Harmony, shaking her head and smiling. She then looked over toward Vanessa and asked, "Nessa, who's this you want me to see?"

"Come on!" Vanessa said, waving at Alinna as she walked around the back end of the Phantom, entered the front gate, and opened the door to the house.

Following both Vanessa and Harmony inside the house, Alinna was surprised to see that the inside was actually fixed up nicely. She looked toward the kitchen just as a middle-aged black woman walked out of it.

"Mary . . . get Keisha, Maxine, and Kyree for me," Vanessa told the woman, receiving a smile right before she walked off and headed upstairs.

"Who the hell was that?" Alinna asked while staring at the woman as she headed upstairs.

"This Keisha's mom, Alinna," Harmony answered as she started walking toward the kitchen.

"Hold on!" Alinna said, looking from Harmony to Vanessa with a balled-up face. "What the hell going on in here, Vanessa? Why the fuck is we in some woman's house, and who the hell is Keisha and them?"

"Just re—" Vanessa stated, just as Keisha and then Maxine came down the stairs behind each other.

"What's up, Vanessa?" Keisha said as she stopped on the bottom step and noticed the Spanish female and the white boy. "Who's the white boy with Alinna?"

"You know me?" Alinna asked the young, light-skinned female while staring at her.

"Who don't know you?" Maxine spoke up. "Everybody knows the wife of Dante Blackwell, with his too fine-ass self."

29

Looking from one young woman to the other, Alinna realized she was looking at twins. She then looked back at Vanessa and asked, "Who the fuck is this?"

"That's Keisha, with the nose ring, in front of you . . . and that's Maxine," Vanessa told Alinna, as she nodded to both girls. She then looked up at Kyree who came walking down the steps. She smirked and said, "And this is Kyree. He's both Keisha and Maxine's older brother."

Looking the young guy over, Alinna shook her head and turned to step away from Kyree and over to Vanessa, only to catch Kyree's hand reaching out to grab at her arm. In a blur, she saw James move, and Kyree was pinned facedown on the ground.

"Damn!" both Keisha and Maxine said together after seeing their brother being taken down by the white boy with Alinna.

Maxine smiled at James as she asked, "Alinna, who's the white boy?"

"Allow me to introduce James," Alinna told them while nodding to James to release Kyree. "He my personal bodyguard and Dante's best friend."

"How can we become best friends too?" Maxine asked flirtatiously as she walked up to James with a smile.

"Now that we know each other," Vanessa started, smiling at Alinna, "I wanted you to meet the three of them because, first, Kyree is going to be my new lieutenant at the two new spots out in Hollywood, Florida."

"You sure?" Alinna asked, looking back to Kyree, who stood rubbing his left shoulder and staring angrily at James.

"Don't let Kyree make you think bad about him, Alinna," Keisha spoke up for her brother before adding, "He just stupid when it comes to the women he picks."

"He rather James than Dante," Alinna replied before looking back toward Vanessa and asking, "So what's up with the two ladies, Vanessa?"

"Well, as for Keisha and Maxine . . . ," Vanessa said, smiling as she looked at the twins, "Let's just say that if Dante was still home, he would love these two."

"What do they do?" Alinna asked, looking back to Keisha and Maxine.

"Other than guns, these lil' hoes is some deadly bitches and love breaking down niggas who think they too gangster," Vanessa explained, still smiling.

"So where you find these three at?" Alinna asked Vanessa while looking over Maxine and then both Keisha and Kyree.

"Harmony knows their uncle," Vanessa answered just as Harmony walked from out of the kitchen eating a stacked-up sandwich, with a bag of Doritos tucked under her arm.

"Harmony . . . what?" Harmony asked, mouth filled with food.

Ignoring Harmony and looking back at the twins, Alinna said, "Alright . . . I'ma see what's up, Kyree. But you get one try. I don't accept anything but the best because that's what me, Dante, and this family build this family off of. You sure you're ready to handle what you're being offered?"

"I'm ready when you and Vanessa ready," Kyree told Alinna, showing a cocky-like smile.

"What about us?" Keisha asked, getting Alinna's attention.

"My sister say you two know how to handle your business, so until an issue arrives where I may need the two of your services, I'll put you on security working directly with James," Alinna told both Keisha and Maxine. "That means that James is now your boss. Is there a problem with that?"

31

"None!" Keisha answered.

"Definitely not . . . !" Maxine answered with a big smile as she wrapped her arms around James's waist.

Alinna smiled as she watched Maxine with James. She then turned toward Vanessa and said, "Put 'em on, Nessa. All three of 'em, and we'll discuss payment later."

"Where you going?" Harmony asked as she was finishing off her Doritos.

"I've got some stuff to take care of, and then I gotta meet with Dante's lawyer," Alinna told Harmony as she started toward the front door.

*　　*　　*

"Dante!" Officer Cook called out from her desk after fishing her paperwork. Once her shift started and the unit were still in their bunks waiting for the floor to be opened to allow the inmates to watch TV and move around, she waved Dante over to her desk. She then yelled out, "Fall's open. Keep the noise down."

Hearing Officer Cook, Dante left his bunk and headed to the officer's desk, ignoring the stares he received from some of the inmates. He stopped in front of the desk, saw her smile, and he said, "What's up, Kerri?"

"How you doing, Dante?"

"I'm doing what I do."

"So what's this about you beating up some guy inside the restroom?" she asked, smiling harder at Dante.

Shrugging his shoulders carelessly, Dante calmly said, "I ain't hear nothing about no fight."

"You a trip, Dante!" Kerri said, laughing lightly as she shook her head. She then continued, "So you gonna be my trustee?"

32

"You offering a job, Kerri?" Dante asked, staring into her brown eyes.

"Hold on!" she told Dante. She then called out to an inmate named Travis, waving him over to her desk.

"What's up, Officer Cook?" the inmate asked as he stopped next to the officer's desk.

"Travis, this is Dante Blackwell . . ."

"I know who Dante is," Travis said, interrupting Kerri. "Who doesn't know who Dante is?"

"That's good," Kerri replied, but then said, "Well, from now on, Travis . . . you, Chris, and both Tony and Jim now work for Dante. He's going to be my new houseman."

Watching the change in Travis's expression as homeboy looked from Kerri to him, Dante held dude's eyes a moment until dude turned and walked angrily away. Dante shifted his eyes back toward Kerri and asked, "How you go from trustee to houseman?"

Shrugging her shoulders now, smiling again up at Dante, Kerri asked, "So you accepting the job, right?"

"Whatever," Dante answered before asking, "How this whole houseman shit goes, though? Is it just your shift or all three shifts?"

"All three shifts. Why?"

"Your boy Jefferson ain't really feeling me, so I'm sure it's gonna be something with homeboy when he finds out what's up with this houseman shit."

"Fuck him!" Kerri replied in a lowered voice. "His ass don't run shit. I'm the senior officer in this unit, and his ass just don't like you because what they say happened with you and his brother."

"What you mean with me and his brother?" Dante asked, face balled up in a confused expression. "Who the fuck is his brother?"

"Everybody call him Prince, but his—"

"So Prince is this nigga Jefferson's brother, huh?" Dante said, cutting off Kerri. He then asked, "How you know they brothers?"

"Because I used to mess with Jefferson some time ago," Kerri admitted. "He introduced me to Prince as his girlfriend, and Prince as his brother. His big brother."

Nodding his head from the information that Kerri just gave him, Dante had a quick thought. But realizing the problems he was facing, he focused back on Kerri and said, "You still fuck with this nigga Jefferson?"

"Hell naw . . . his ass been over," Kerri answered with much attitude. "His ass used to beat up on me and even pulled a knife on me one night after work. Fuck his ass!"

"I think we may be able to help each other," Dante told her, smirking his devilish-like smile.

"How?" Kerri asked, staring hard into Dante's eyes and seeing the smile he had on his face.

"We'll discuss that later," Dante told her, winking his eye at her.

5

Alinna was sitting in the den back at the penthouse talking with Natalie when James entered followed by Jonathan King, the attorney. Natalie waved off Gomez, who stood at the sight of the middle-aged white man. Alinna stood up from her seat on the couch and held out her hand. She spoke: "Thank you for coming, Mr. King. Allow me to introduce you to Natalie Saldana."

"Ms. Saldana . . . ," Mr. King said, releasing Alinna's hand and taking Natalie's and shaking it gently. He continued, "Mr. Blackwell has told me about you, and after our meeting now, I would like to discuss a few things with you concerning matters of you and your unborn child, for which Mr. Blackwell has begun setting up plans."

"That will be fine, sir," Natalie replied, smiling at the thought of Dante planning for her and their child.

"Please, Mr. King," Alinna spoke up, motioning to the attorney. "Please, have a seat."

"Thank you," Mr. King replied as he took a seat on the sofa across from both Alinna and Natalie. He set down the briefcase he was carrying onto a glass coffee table. He opened it, pulled out a brown folder, and then handed it over to Alinna. "This is what's been filed on Mr. Blackwell, and if you turn to the third page, you'll see everyone who's involved in Mr. Blackwell's case, as well as the arresting officers."

"Dante was telling me something that the case may be turning into a federal case," Alinna told the attorney while looking through the file.

"There's a big chance that the case will, Mrs. Blackwell, considering the fact that not only is Mr. Blackwell being charged with murder of a law enforcement officer who was a captain for the Miami-Dade Police Department, but he's also being charged with murder of a federal agent as well," Mr. King explained to Alinna, glancing over at Natalie as both women sat looking inside the file.

"Why's there only two names on here for the arresting officers?" Alinna asked as she looked up at the attorney. "This says that Sergeant Aaron Banks and Detective Howard Fuller from the MDPD were the only two arresting officers."

"Were they not, Mrs. Blackwell?" Mr. King asked, staring at Alinna with questioning eyes.

"Hell . . . !" Alinna started but then paused as she thought about something. "You know what, Mr. King, maybe this is right. I may have been looking for something to hold onto and hope for."

"That's understandable," Mr. King replied, catching the change in expression on Alinna's face as she changed up what she was about to say.

Continuing the meeting with the attorney and even writing down a few things from the file before Mr. King left, Alinna walked him to the door, thanking him and exchanging goodbyes. Security then escorted Mr. King to the elevator. Alinna closed the door behind her, locked it, and then turned and faced James. "Something's not right, James."

"Explain," James told her, following Alinna back to the den where Natalie and Gomez sat talking to each other and waiting.

"James, you were there just like I was there when Dante turned himself in," Alinna told James as they stood in the entrance to the den. She stared at him and continued, "Whoever the fuck Sergeant Aaron Banks and Detective Howard Fuller are, they weren't the ones who arrested Dante. It was Paul and that bitch, Monica."

"Who's Monica and Paul?" Natalie spoke up, getting both Alinna's and James's attention.

"It's the wife and partner of the DEA agent Dante is accused of killing," James said, drawing everyone's attention to him.

"Something's not right with this whole case," Alinna said, speaking up again. "This bitch Monica said she was going to try and bury Dante for killing Alex."

"When's he supposed to call?" Natalie asked, looking at her Rolex watch.

"He should be calling by 10:00 p.m.," Alinna replied while thinking about what Dante was talking about when he said something wasn't right with this case.

* * *

Dante hung out at the officer's desk talking with Kerri until she finally closed the floor by 11:00 p.m. Dante then turned out the unit's lights at Kerri's request. He walked back over to the desk and then began cleaning up around the office area while Kerri started on her paperwork.

"Here!" Kerri said as she dug out some latex gloves.

Taking the gloves, Dante walked off and headed inside the restroom to the supply closet to get the broom.

"What you need us to do, boss man?" Dante heard as he looked back over his shoulder to see the big man, Jim, who was one of the trustees. He looked past the big man to his right to see no one else. Dante looked back to Jim and asked, "Where are the others at?"

"Tony said he was coming, but the nigga Travis still feeling some type of way about you taking his houseman position," Jim explained to Dante.

"Fuck him . . . !" Dante said as he handed Jim a push broom.

Dante spent a little more than five minutes with Jim cleaning up the unit and bagging up the trash, when Kerri whispered to him to go to the restroom. Dante said nothing as he walked off after first tossing the trash inside of the large trash bag that went out with the breakfast in the morning.

Nodding to Jim as the big man headed toward his bunk, Dante entered the restroom and walked over to the sink area.

He was washing his face with cold water when Kerri walked into the restroom carrying a white plastic bag. Dante left the sink running, dried his face with his jail-issued shirt, and then turned his back to the sink counter as Kerri handed him the plastic bag.

"That's something I picked up from the Rib House off 22nd Avenue," Kerri told Dante. She then pulled her cell phone from her pocket and handed it over to him. "Be careful with this phone, Dante."

"Do me a favor . . . ," Dante began as he was already dialing Alinna's number. "Go get the nigga Jim and tell him to come holla at me real quick."

"Hello," Alinna answered on the start of the second ring.

"What's up, shorty? You miss me?"

"Dante, who's phone . . . never mind!" Alinna began, but then thought better of the question she was about to ask him. "I wanna talk to you about these papers that Mr. King brought over to the penthouse."

"Hold up!" Dante stopped her as he picked up the plastic bag with the food inside that Kerri had given him. He held it out to Jim as the big man walked inside the restroom. "This for you, big homie?"

"What's this?" Jim asked, looking at the phone in Dante's hand.

"You eat ribs, right?"

"Hell yeah!"

"There you go," Dante replied, nodding to the bag. "Watch out for me, and I got you on a phone call after I'm done."

"That's what's up, gangster," Jim said, dapping up with Dante with a smile.

"Alinna . . . ," Dante said back into the phone.

"Yeah, baby! Who was you talking to?"

"Nobody. What's up, though? What you found out?"

"I was reading over the file that Mr. King had, and for your arresting officer, they got somebody named Sergeant Aaron Banks and Detective Howard Fuller. Why aren't Monica's and Paul's names anywhere on the file, since they the ones that was behind the investigation. But then I noticed that there was some informant that was also helping with the case."

"What's the informant's name?"

"That's just it, Dante . . . There wasn't a name for the informant," Alinna told him. After a moment passed with no reply from Dante, Alinna prodded, "Dante, what is it? What are you thinking about?"

"I'm not sure yet, Alinna," he answered, trying to play everything inside his head. "Find out who this muthafucker is, Alinna. Find 'im and handle the shit, Alinna!"

Dante spoke with Alinna for a few more minutes before hanging up. He then called another phone number.

"What go on? Who this be?" Wesley answered after two rings.

"What's up, Rastaman?" Dante said, smiling at the sound of Wesley's voice.

"Blood clot . . . me rude boy, brethren, is on the blood clot phone. What go on, Dante?"

"Wesley, I need you to handle something for me, mom. You got me?"

"Every time, my brethren. What you need, rude boy?"

After explaining to Wesley about Officer Jefferson and telling him what he wanted him to do, Dante hung up the phone with a smirk on his face. However, his smirk quickly faded as thoughts of the informant Alinna told him about entered back into his mind.

* * *

Alinna called Greg Wilson immediately after hanging up with Dante. She spent five minutes on the phone explaining to the business associate what she needed concerning information on who the informant was in Dante's case. She further explained that she had $50,000 for him once he came up with the information.

Hanging up with the private investigator, Alinna then called Natalie.

"Hello!"

"Natalie, it's Alinna."

"You spoke with Dante?"

"I spoke with him, and I also just got off the phone with this investigator that works for Dante named Greg—"

"Greg Wilson," Natalie finished, interrupting Alinna. "I know who Greg is. He used to work for my father, but now he works for Dante. What did Dante say?"

"He wants me to find out who this informant is that's on the case, but I also want to find out exactly what's going on with Dante's case and why Monica's name isn't showing up when she was the main person behind Dante's arrest."

"I'm going to call my mother and see if she can help us out with this," Natalie told Alinna. "Hopefully she can help. I'll call you back tomorrow."

"Call me after 11:00 a.m. I got a meeting at 10:00 with a buyer."

"Alright, Alinna."

Hanging up with Natalie and then laying the cell phone on top of the bedside dresser, Alinna sat on the side of her bed a moment, trying to put everything together inside her head. In the end, she decided to get in contact with Angela.

6

Alinna was unable to sleep most of the night, so she decided to get up early and handle some business runs. Alinna met with two new major buyers who had flown in from out of state, and then she spoke with both Mr. Sutter and Mr. Goldmen over the phone about the first shipment that was on its way.

Calling Natalie once business for the family was handled, Alinna only reached her voice mail box, so she then called Angela to see if they could meet and talk.

"Hello!"

"Angela, it's Alinna. Are you free to talk?"

"Not really, but what do you want?"

"I wanna ask you a few questions about Dante's case."

"Fuck Dante!" Angela began nastily. "Matter of fact, don't call me about Dante ass no more. Don't call my number period. Whatever happens to Dante's lying ass is good for him!"

Hearing the bitch hang up the phone in her ear, Alinna stared at her cell phone's screen in disbelief and yelled, "No this bitch didn't just hang up on me. I will whoop this hoe ass!"

"What's up, Alinna?" James asked, looking up from his cell after reading the text message that came through.

"That nasty ass bitch had the nerve to hang up in my face, and then she talking that shit about Dante brought whatever happens on himself. She lucky Dante ain't hear that shit! Fuck that bitch!"

"So what's up now?" James asked as he slid his cell phone into his pocket.

"I gotta meet up with the rest of the family and tell them about the new shipment and some new plans I've been thinking about. Call Vanessa and tell her to have the family meet at Auntie Gray's Diner," Alinna told James while trying Natalie's number again.

* * *

"What they say?" Dante asked as he walked up in front of the officer's desk where Kerri was just hanging up the phone with her face all balled up in anger. "They still ain't sent nobody to fill in for Officer Jefferson yet?"

"They sending up somebody now," Kerri said, waving her hand dismissively at two inmates who were approaching her desk. "This just like some shit Jefferson's ass would do."

"Relax . . . This may just be a good sign right here," Dante told her, winking his eye at Kerri.

Hearing the unit's door being opened and seeing her girl Gina walking inside the unit, Kerri stood up from behind the desk and hugged her when she walked up. "Officer Harris! Girl . . . What you doing here?"

"This is where they got me at since Officer Jefferson quit," Gina told her friend, but then noticed who was standing in front of the officer's desk. "Dante Blackwell . . . So this is where they put you at."

"For the moment," Dante replied, but then looked to Kerri and said, "I'ma see you tonight, right?"

"I'ma be here," she replied, smiling as she stood watching him walk off from the desk.

"Kerri Cook!" Gina cried, staring at Kerri smiling. "You mean to tell me you know Dante Blackwell, girl?"

"We're friends, Gina," Kerri told her girl, smiling as she picked up her lunch bag from the table top.

"Yeah, before you go . . . ," Gina added, stopping Kerri as she started for the door, "You gonna find out, but I'ma tell you now. Jefferson in the hospital at Parkway. This morning he got beat up really bad and put in the hospital. He had his sister call in and say that he quit."

Surprised at the news, Kerri found herself looking over at Dante, only to meet his eyes and catch the wink he gave her.

* * *

"Look who it is, ya'll!" Tony T said jokingly at seeing Alinna as she entered the diner with James. They both headed over to the large, round table where Tony T and the rest of the family were seated.

"What's up, ya'll?" Alinna said, smiling as she walked up to the table where the group was sitting. She hugged both Harmony and Amber and then pushed each of the guys upside their heads as she took the seat next to Vanessa. James allowed her to sit down first, and then he sat down beside her to her right.

"How my baby doing, Alinna?" Amber asked, speaking up first before they could get into the more serious matters she knew they all were there for.

"Who you talking about?" Vanessa asked with a smile. "You talking about D.J., who you stay spoiling, or his daddy?"

"You almost sound jealous!" Amber told Vanessa, rolling her eyes as she looked back at Alinna. "How is Dante doing up in that place?"

"Dante doing what Dante does best, girl!" Alinna answered, sucking her teeth with a smile. "Well, ya'll . . . listen. I spoke with both new connects . . ."

Alinna then stopped in the middle of what she was just trying to tell the others when the waitress walked up to the table. Alinna waited while everyone ordered a meal.

"Damn, Harmony! All that food you just ordered," Tony T said after the waitress walked off. "What . . . you pregnant or something?"

"Shut up, Tony T!" Harmony said, pushing him upside the head. "Go ahead, Alinna. What was you just saying, girl."

Alinna shook her head and smiled. She then continued what she was saying, explaining that she spoke with the new connects, Mr. Goldmen and Mr. Sutter. She then went into explaining the new business ideas she came up with and that she wanted to see what the family thought about the ideas.

"Hold up a second, ya'll!" Alinna told everyone at the table, hearing her cell phone ring. She dug out her iPhone from her Gucci bag and saw Greg Wilson's name and phone number. "Ya'll hold on for a second. I'ma be right back."

Leaving her table and the others, Alinna walked to the front entrance and out of the diner as she answered the investigator's call.

"Mrs. Blackwell, how are you? This is Greg W—"

"I know who this is," Alinna said, cutting him off. "What do you have for me, Mr. Wilson?"

"Well, Mrs. Blackwell, I have both good and bad news."

"Give me the good news first."

"Well, I've found the addresses and information on the two detectives who are listed in Mr. Blackwell's case as the arresting officers. I can give you all I have now if you want?"

Looking back and seeing James a few feet away, Alinna motioned him over. She then said to Mr. Wilson, "So what do you have on this informant thing?"

"That's the bad news I told you I also had," Wilson replied. "I looked and asked around, and seeing that everyone's talking about this case, nobody's talking about any informant. It's like nobody knows anything about this informant I'm asking about. Whoever this person is, everyone's going out of their way to really protect them."

Alinna remained quiet a few minutes, trying to control her emotions before she motioned for James to get something to write with. She then said to Greg, "Give me everything you've got on the two detectives, Mr. Wilson."

Alinna repeated the addresses of both detectives so James could write them down. She stood up and listened to everything else that Wilson had to say. She then hung up the phone, looked at James, and said, "Looks like we're gonna end up handling this shit by ourselves. Let's get back inside and explain this to the others."

Heading back inside the diner to see that everyone was already eating, both Alinna and James sat down in front of the food. Alinna ignored her meal and then called over to Tony T and Dre: "I need you two to handle something for me."

Telling the others about the informant and everything else Greg Wilson had just told her, Alinna then looked back toward Dre and Tony T and added, "Since Greg Wilson wasn't able to get anything on this informant, I need the two of you to pay these two a visit and bring 'em to me."

* * *

Leaving the diner and the others a little while after talking with them and barely eating her food, Alinna pulled out her cell phone with the intention of calling the twins, Keisha and Maxine, only for the iPhone to go off, ringing inside her hand.

Seeing Natalie's name appear on the screen, Alinna answered, "Natalie, where the hell you been at, girl?"

"Alinna, I'm sorry . . . I just got back in Miami early this morning. I left to go back home, but my mother is here with me now. What have you found out about this informant and Dante's case?"

"Let's meet up and talk. I don't want to talk over the phone."

"Just come to my penthouse. I'll introduce you to my mother when you get here."

"I'll see you in a little while," Alinna replied as she hung up the phone. She then called Keisha.

"What's up? Who's this?"

"Keisha, this Alinna."

"Oh, what's up, Alinna?"

"Look, I got some work for the both of you. I'ma call you and Maxine when I'm ready for the two of you. How's $20,000 for convincing someone to give up some information?"

"Not a problem," Keisha answered before adding, "Hold on. Is James next to you?"

"Yeah, why?"

"Maxine wants to talk to him. Hold on."

Smiling as she handed the phone to James, Alinna said, "You've got a phone call."

* * *

Hearing Gomez call her name as she and her mother sat talking and discussing her father, Dominic, Natalie turned her attention away from her mother. She looked toward the front door from inside the sitting room just as Alinna and James walked in. Gomez then shut the front door.

"Alinna . . . !" Natalie cried, smiling as she stood up beside her mother. She turned to Alinna and embraced her, pulled back, and then said, "Alinna, meet my mother, Carmen Saldana."

"Mrs. Saldana," she said, taking the older Spanish woman's hand. Alinna found her mother to be surprisingly beautiful and much younger than she most likely was. "It's good meeting you, Mrs. Saldana."

"Please, call me Carmen," she replied, looking Alinna over. "I see that our Dante has an attraction to Hispanic women. You're very beautiful, Alinna."

"Thank you, Mrs. . . . . I mean Carmen," Alinna corrected herself.

"Let's all sit down," Natalie suggested, waving both her mother and Alinna to be seated.

"So, Alinna . . . ," Carmen started once the three of them were seated. She noticed Gomez and James walking into the kitchen before focusing back on Alinna and saying, "My daughter was just explaining to me about the issue the two of you have been dealing with concerning some informant that's supposed to speak out against Dante and the murder case he's being charged with. Am I right to guess that you are still unaware of whom this informant is?"

"You're correct," Alinna answered before quickly adding, "I've already started steps to find out who this informant is."

"And once you find out who this informant is, will you be handling things on a permanent level?" Carmen asked, staring directly into Alinna's eyes.

Understanding loud and clear what was being asked, Alinna slowly let out a small smile and responded, "That's exactly what I was thinking."

* * *

"There's the house right there!" Tony T said, pointing toward the green and white house. He and Dre drove past it just as a white SUV Kia Sorento was pulling into the driveway.

Not responding, Dre continued driving right past the house. Dre then made a complete drive around the block, only to end up pulling right in front of the house.

"Dre, what the fuck is you doing, nigga?" Tony T asked as Dre shut off the Land Rover.

"Exactly what Dante would do," Dre answered as he was climbing from the Land Rover, shutting the driver's door behind him.

"What the fuck . . . !" Tony T shouted as he sat staring at Dre through the window of the Land Rover. He shook his head but quickly climbed from the SUV and followed behind Dre. "Bro, what the fuck is you planning on doing?"

Dre didn't bother answering Tony T as he stepped up onto the porch of the house into which he saw the Kia pull. Dre then knocked on the door loud enough to make sure he was heard.

Hearing the door being unlocked a few moments later, Dre stood in front of the door as it slowly swung open and a nice-looking middle-aged woman stood there.

"Hello, can I help you?" she asked, looking first at the well-built man and then toward the brown-skinned man with diamonds the size of her pinky finger in both his ears.

"Howard Fuller lives here, right?" Dre asked the woman, staring directly into her eyes.

"Yes, he does. May I . . ."

Dre caught the woman off guard as he grabbed her around the throat and squeezed hard enough to keep her from screaming. He then walked into the house, with Tony T following behind him and locking the front door behind them.

"I'ma release your throat, but if you scream or make any noise, I will kill you. Nod if you understand me," Dre told the woman. She slowly nodded her head. As he released her, he continued, "Okay! I want to know where your husband is now?"

"W-w-work," she answered, staring up at the huge guy with fear showing in her eyes.

"This is what I want you to do. Call your husband and tell him there's an emergency and that you need him to hurry home now. But if you warn him at any time, your husband will come home to a dead wife. Now call your husband!" Dre ordered the woman, continuing to stare directly into her eyes.

7

D re heard the front door unlock and be jerked open forcefully. He then heard a slight deep voice call out, "Nicole." Dre was seated on the couch in the front room next to the detective's wife when Detective Fuller rushed inside.

"Nicole! What's . . . what the fuck?" Detective Fuller yelled upon seeing his wife tied up and her mouth taped. He then shifted his eyes over to the man seated next to her as he went to reach for his service-issued gun, only to freeze once he felt the barrel of a gun pressed to the side of his head. "Shit!"

"How's it going, Detective?" Tony T asked as he removed the gun from the detective's side holster and slid it into the front of his jeans. He then patted down the detective and found a back gun in an ankle holster.

"What the hell's going on? Who the fuck are you two, and why the fuck are you guys inside my house?" Detective Fuller questioned once the second guy walked around in his line of view.

"Good to see you again, Detective Fuller," Dre said as he sat relaxed. "I see you don't remember us, but someone wants to have a few words with you."

Staring at the big man a few minutes and trying to figure out where he was supposed to recognize him from, the detective looked back at Dre and saw him on the cell phone and heard the name Alinna.

Dre stared straight at the detective while talking to Alinna, who was telling him the location of where to take the detective.

"So you work for Alinna Rodriguez, Dante Blackwell's bitch?" Detective Fuller asked Dre as he hung up the cell phone.

Slowly smiling at the detective, Dre stood up from his seat and said, "I'll make sure I let her know you think she's a bitch once we get where we're going. Let's go, Detective."

* * *

Alinna hung up the phone with Dre and smiled after hearing the first piece of good news since Dante turned himself in. She then looked back at Natalie and her mother and said, "Looks like things are starting to change for the better, ladies."

"What's happened, Alinna?" Natalie asked, smiling just from seeing Alinna's grin.

"We're all about to go see someone who's going to start helping us out with what's going on with Dante's case and who this informant really is," Alinna began to explain. She then stood up from her seat and called out for James. Immediately, James, Gomez, and a darker-skinned Spanish man dressed in a suit all left the kitchen and walked into the living room where the women were sitting.

"What's wrong, Alinna?" James asked calmly but alertly.

"We're leaving to meet with Dre and Tony T at my old stash house," she told James. She then looked back toward Natalie and Carmen and said, "The both of you can ride with me while James rides with Gomez and . . ."

"Carlos!" Carmen spoke up, finishing for Alinna, smiling at the younger woman.

They all left Natalie's penthouse and made their way to Alinna's Phantom. The three women were surrounded by a huge team of security. Alinna introduced the driver to Carmen and then reintroduced Natalie. She gave him the address to where they were going, and then the three women climbed inside.

"Who exactly are we going to see, Alinna?" Carmen asked as the back door was shut.

"His name is Howard Fuller, and he's one of the detectives named on Dante's case as an arresting office," Alinna told Carmen just as the Phantom began to move forward. She pulled out her cell phone and told both Carmen and Natalie to hold on for a minute while she made a call.

"What's up? Who is this?" Keisha answered on the second ring.

"Keisha, this Alinna. Meet me at this address," Alinna told the young woman on the other end of the line. "It's time for you and Maxine to get to work."

*   *   *

"Blackwell, come here!" Kerri called as soon as she sat down at her desk and Officer Harris had left. She watched as Dante stood up from his bunk and started walking toward her desk.

"You plan on doing your paperwork before you start wasting time talking to me?" Dante asked as he stopped in front of the officer desk and caught a smile on Kerri's face.

"Boy . . . I said Eddie."

"Who?"

"Officer Jefferson," Kerri told him in a lowered voice before saying, "Who the hell you get to beat the shit out of him like that?"

"You brought your phone with you?" Dante asked, ignoring her question.

"Yeah, I brought it. But I also bought you a prepaid phone with some minutes on it already. You can use it and throw it away if anything was to happen," Kerri explained. "Why? You need it now?"

"I just need to let my family know some stuff I been putting together in my head, and I don't wanna talk over the unit's phone," Dante explained as Kerri was already digging inside of her lunch bag.

"Ahh, Ms. Cook," Travis said as he walked up to the desk.

"What Travis?" Kerri asked with an attitude.

"I need to talk to you about something real quick," he told her as he cut his eyes over toward Dante.

"I'll talk to you later after I open the floor," Kerri told the inmate, waving him away. She then turned toward Dante as Travis walked away and mumbled to him, "I'll leave the phone in back of the handicap toilet in the backend of the restroom."

Nodding his head in response, Dante turned around and walked back to his bunk. He sat down and leaned back against the metal rail of the head of the bunk.

He watched Kerri stand up at her desk and walk through the unit, making her way toward the restroom. Dante sat for a few more minutes until Kerri returned from the restroom and called out his name and waved him over to her.

Leaving his bunk again and making his way over to Kerri's desk, Dante stopped in front of her and said, "What's up, Officer Cook?"

"Do me a favor, Blackwell. Clean up the restroom area for me, please. It smells like piss in there," Kerri said loud enough so most of the inmates could hear her.

"Yeah, alright," Dante replied before turning around and calling out to Jim. Nodding to the big man, Dante said, "Come help me clean up this restroom real quick."

Kerri handed two sets of latex gloves to Dante and then nodded to the big man, who followed Dante into the restroom. In a lowered voice, Dante said, "Look out, big homie. I'ma bless you tonight."

"Handle ya business, boss man!" Jim said as he took position where he could see who was coming into the restroom.

After finding the phone on the side of the handicapped toilet as Kerri as directed, Dante sat down on the toilet and turned on the phone.

Seeing the phone's alert of 4,000 minutes, Dante smirked as he reminded himself to look out for Kerri. He then dialed Alinna's number.

"Hello!" Alinna answered after three rings.

"Everything alright, shorty?" Dante asked after hearing the tone of Alinna's voice when she answered.

"Hey, baby. You've got good timing," Alinna said in a much happier voice. "You're not going to guess who I'm having a few words with."

"Who that?"

"Wait a minute."

Waiting on Alinna, only to hear loud screaming after a moment, Dante balled up his face and then called out to her.

"Yeah, baby!" Alinna answered, yelling a little over the screaming in the background.

"What the fuck is going on?" Dante asked, sounding and feeling a little worried. "Alinna, are you alright? Where the fuck are you?"

"Dante, I'm fine," Alinna answered, not wanting to say much over the phone. However, once Dante told her that he was talking on a prepaid phone, Alinna explained further.

"So who the hell got dude screaming like he a bitch?" Dante asked once Alinna finished telling him about Detective Fuller.

"You've got to meet the twins, Dante," Alinna told him, laughing lightly. "Their names are Keisha and Maxine, and they are amazing, baby. If you could see how they working the hell out of Fuller, you would be proud yourself."

"So what have you found out so far?" Dante asked with a little hope in his voice.

"All he keeps saying is that his partner Sergeant Aaron Banks knows what's going on. He was the one who made the deal with Monica."

"Deal? What deal?"

"Well, from what Fuller says, Monica spoke with Banks and made him an offer . . . and Banks accepted it."

"So where the fuck is this clown Banks?"

"Dre and Tony T handling that now."

"Where's Wesley at?"

"I haven't seen him. Why?" Alinna asked, but then she asked Dante to hold on.

Hearing Alinna ask Keisha if Detective Fuller was dead, Dante called out to Alinna.

"Yeah, Dante!"

"Look, shorty . . . I'ma have to hit you back later tonight because tonight is better than right now. Too many muthafuckers walking around. But tell me something real quick. You speak with Angela lately?"

"Fuck that bitch, Dante!" Alinna said, instantly turning from happy to pissy. "That hoe said you deserve what happens to you and told me not to ask about you to her anymore. She then told me not to call her phone number. She lucky I didn't find and beat her ass for her mouth."

"Don't worry about Angela. I'ma deal with her when I get home," Dante told her, playing back in his head what Alinna just told him that Angela had said about him.

*   *   *

Alinna hung up with Dante, but she could hear the hurt and anger in his voice after she told him what Angela said, which pissed her off again as well. But Alinna focused her attention back on the now unconscious Detective Fuller, who was covered in blood and alcohol.

Maxine had used a doctor's scalpel to make cuts all over Fuller's body as Keisha slowly poured alcohol over all his cuts. After she cut into his penis and alcohol was poured over it, Fuller became unconscious from the pain.

"What now, Alinna?" Natalie asked as she stood beside her mother against the wall in front of where the detective sat tied to a wooden chair.

"We wait for my family to arrive with Sergeant Aaron Banks," Alinna told Natalie. She couldn't help notice the look of satisfaction on Carmen's face as she stood staring at Detective Fuller.

* * *

Dre watched Sergeant Aaron Banks climb inside the driver's seat of a navy-blue Chevy Malibu. A few moments later, he backed out of the parking space in front of the Miami-Dade Police Department building. Dre threw his Land Rover into drive and began to follow the Malibu a few moments later.

Still following the sergeant's car, Dre saw him stop at a red light ten minutes later. Dre stopped his Land Rover a few feet away behind two cars, which allowed Tony T to get out of the SUV. Dre then switched lanes and pulled directly alongside the Malibu as he looked over and saw the sergeant light up a cigarette.

Hitting the Land Rover's horn caused the sergeant to look over at the Land Rover. Dre lowered the dark-tinted window and looked over at the sergeant just as Tony T opened up the sergeant's front passenger seat door and slid in.

"What the . . . ?"

"Shut the fuck up and drive the car!" Tony T ordered Sergeant Banks, pressing his banger into the sergeant's ribs.

"Who the hell are—"

Smashing the sergeant in the mouth with a right hook, Tony T cut him off again from talking. He then repeated, "Shut the fuck up and drive the fucking car. The light is green, bitch!"

Doing as he was told, Sergeant Banks followed Dre's SUV until Tony T told him to pull into a Walmart parking lot beside the Land Rover.

"If you think because we inside a parking lot I won't dead ya ass, act like you wanna get stupid and yell or make a run for it, and I'll drop your ass wherever the fuck you stand. Now get the fuck out of the car!" Tony T told the sergeant as he was also opening his own car door.

Dre and Tony T got Sergeant Banks into the back of the SUV. Tony T did a quick wipe-down of the sergeant's Malibu where he had sat and the parts of the car he had touched. He then returned to the back of the SUV with Banks.

Sergeant Banks recognized the driver, but he couldn't remember from where. He was in deep thought about what he could do, when Dre finally spoke: "It's good seeing you again, Sergeant Banks. I'm sure you're wondering where we're going, so I'll tell you now before you even have to ask. Someone wants to talk with you, and that's where we're going."

"Who wants to talk to . . . ?"

"Shut the fuck up!" Tony T said, cutting off the sergeant again.

Sergeant Banks gave a pissed off look toward Tony T, which caused him to smile at the sergeant. Tony T followed this with a punch to his mouth, which caused the sergeant's head to snap backward from the blow.

*   *   *

Alinna hung up the phone with Dre, who had just called to tell her that he was pulling inside the apartment's parking lot out front. Alinna called out to Keisha, who was standing out on the balcony talking on her phone. Maxine was with James a few feet away, talking in a whispered voice. Alinna motioned both girls over to her.

"What's up, Alinna?" Keisha asked as she and her sister walked up.

"You two get ready to work. Dre and Tony T just got here with the other guy," Alinna told the twins.

She then looked back over to Natalie and her mother and asked, "What's up, Natalie?"

"Alinna, we need to talk," Natalie told her, only for Carmen to speak up and say, "My husband is here, and he wants us to meet him back at our place. Natalie will call you later."

Walking both women to the front door, with James just a few steps behind them, Alinna reached to unlock the door, when suddenly she heard a knock on the door. A second later, James jumped in front of her gripping his gun, with both Carlos and Gomez guarding Natalie and Carmen.

"It's Dre and Tony T, James," Alinna told him as James unlocked the door with his left hand while holding the barrel of his burner up against the back of the door as he opened it to see Dre's face.

Smiling and shaking her head once James looked back at her, Alinna stepped to the side as first Dre walked into the apartment followed by Sergeant Banks. She met the sergeant's eyes, which grew in size once he recognized who he was looking at.

Alinna walked Carmen and Natalie out to her Phantom and told her driver what was happening. The women said their goodbyes, hugged, and then Alinna reminded Natalie to call her later as the driver took off.

Alinna headed back up to the apartment, only to hear muffled screams as soon as James opened the apartment door. Alinna entered and walked into the front room to see Maxine standing in front of Sergeant Banks, using her scalpel to peel off the skin on his chest while Dre held his hand over the sergeant's mouth.

Standing with Alinna and watching, James leaned over and asked in a lowered voice, "You think you'll be able to figure this all out before Dante has to stand before the judge?"

"I'm not letting Dante step foot inside of a prison, James," Alinna replied. She then walked up beside Maxine and touched the one twin's back, which caused Maxine to pause in mid-peel.

"So, Sergeant Banks, let's not make this an all-day-and-night thing here. Tell me about this deal you and Agent Monica Martin made concerning Dante Blackwell's case and who's the informant on this case?" Alinna asked while nodding for Dre to release his hand from over the sergeant's mouth. But as soon as Dre took his hand down, the sergeant spit onto the front of Alinna's Dolce & Gabbana blouse.

"Fuck you, bitch! I hope they fry the muthafuckers!" Sergeant Banks screamed, only for Dre to slam his fist into the side of the sergeant's jaw, knocking him out cold.

"Dre!" Alinna cried, staring hard at him before a smile appeared. "Did you have to knock him out?"

"I wasn't trying to," Dre apologized with a shrug and smirk.

Shaking her head, Alinna looked over at Keisha, who stood a few feet away texting on her phone, and asked, "Keisha, where's Detective Fuller?"

"He's tied up and inside the bathroom with his wife," Keisha answered without looking up from her phone.

Shaking her head again, Alinna looked back at Maxine and asked, "You alright with being here for some time?"

"This where the job is . . . plus, he's still here, so I'm fine," Maxine answered, smiling and nodding toward James.

"Good, because it looks like it's going to be a long night," Alinna said as she pulled out her cell phone.

8

Alinna made it back to the penthouse a little after 10:00 p.m., leaving Dre and Tony T to handle Sergeant Banks, Detective Fuller, and Fuller's wife. Alinna barely made it through the front door when she was attacked by her son, Dante Jr.

"What are you still doing up, D.J.?" Alinna asked, smiling as she picked up her quickly growing son, first hugging him, then kissing his cheek.

"Stop!" D.J. cried, laughing as he pulled away from his mother.

"Hello, Ms. Rodriguez," Rose, the housekeeper, said, smiling as she walked out into the front room just as D.J. was turning to take off, only to run straight into her.

"D.J.!" Alinna said, raising her voice just enough to cause her son to stop where he was and turn to look at her. She then continued, "You need to find your way to bed and be there when I get there."

Forcing herself to ignore the look he was giving her, with eyes exactly like his father's, she watched as he slowly turned and began walking in the direction of the master bedroom—the room in which the two of them began sleeping after they moved into the penthouse, before Dante went to jail.

"He reminds so much of Mr. Blackwell," Rose said, smiling as she also stood there watching D.J. disappear around the corner on way to the master bedroom.

"I was just thinking the same thing, Rose," Alinna replied as she started toward the den.

"Would you like to eat, Ms. Rod—"

"Not right now, Rose," Alinna told the older woman but then looked back and said, "And Rose . . . I thought we had an understanding that you are also a part of this family and you are to call me Alinna like everyone else."

"I remember, Alinna," Rose replied, smiling at Alinna. "I will put a plate inside the oven when you are ready to eat. Tell Mr. Grant that his plate will be inside the oven as well."

"Thank you, Rose," Alinna said, sitting down on the sofa and sighing deeply, only to hear her cell phone go off, ringing from inside her bag.

Digging out her phone, she saw that it was Natalie calling.

"Hello!"

"Alinna, it's Natalie."

"I know. Is everything alright?"

"My mother and father are at my father's penthouse, but everything is alright," Natalie told her. But then she asked, "What have you found out after we left you? Did you get any answered questions?"

"I got . . . ," hearing the line beep and looking at the screen, Alinna didn't recognize the number. She told Natalie to hold on a second.

"What's up, shorty?"

"Dante, baby! Hold on. Natalie's on the other line. I'll put her on a conference call," Alinna told Dante, connecting the calls. "Natalie, you there?"

"Yes, I'm here."

"Dante, baby. You there?"

"Yeah!"

"Oh my God! Papi, I miss you so much," Natalie cried at hearing Dante's voice. "Are you okay in there?"

"I'm good, Natalie," Dante told her. "How you holding up, though?"

"I'm going crazy, Dante. I want you out of there, and both me and Alinna have been doing everything we can think of to get you home."

"I'm glad to hear you and Alinna are handling business out there," Dante told her before he called out to Alinna.

"Yes, Dante," Alinna answered as she stretched out across the sofa.

"You alright, shorty?"

"Yes, baby. I'm fine, Dante," she replied. "I talked to Wesley earlier. He asked me to tell you that he took care of what you asked him to handle. You wanna tell me what Wesley's talking about, since he won't?"

"It ain't nothing. What you got for me, though?"

Smiling at the response Dante gave her and the smooth way he changed the subject, Alinna decided to leave the matter of what Wesley had handled for Dante alone. Instead, she decided to just answer his question: "I had a talk with both arresting officers on your case. It took some time, but the only thing I was able to find out was that Sergeant Banks and Monica made a deal. She let him have all claims to the arrest against you, since your arrest was supposedly a major one."

"Why would she do that, since she was so ready to get at me about her supposed husband and partner?" Dante asked, sounding a little confused.

"From what the sergeant told me, Monica told him that part of the deal she made was that you would either get a life sentence or the death penalty for killing Alex and Captain Whitehead, but also that you had a more desperate enemy that was after you," Alinna broke down, explaining for Dante.

"Dante, you can't think of any enemies you may have that may just be working with the police with this case?" Natalie asked him.

"Unless they telling on Dante from the grave, then I don't see that happening, Natalie," Alinna told her. "Dante doesn't have any living enemies."

"Alinna, listen . . . ," Dante spoke up. "I want you to get on finding out who this so-called enemy is that Banks says Monica told him about."

"I'm already taking care of that. I've got Greg Wilson looking up whatever he can find on Monica so we can find her and see what she can tell us."

"Let me know what's up with that," Dante told her. "Yeah, also, I want you to handle something for me. It's this female I want you to call and have her meet up with you. Give her $10,000, and let her know it's my way of saying thank you."

"Who is she?" Alinna and Natalie asked in unison.

"Relax! She's the one who's been making it able for me to handle a few things from inside here," Dante explained to both women.

"Dante, don't make me hurt you," Alinna told him . . . with Natalie adding, "Please don't, Dante."

Alinna continued talking with both Dante and Natalie until Dante had to hang up. She continued discussing a few things with Natalie until her phone rang and she saw that Vanessa was calling.

"Natalie, let me call you back later. I need to answer my other line real quick," Alinna told her, sitting up on the sofa.

"I'ma just call you tomorrow," Natalie told Alinna. "I've also got a few things I want to handle."

Immediately after hanging up with Natalie, Alinna switched her line over to Vanessa. "Hey, Nessa. What's up, girl?"

"You was on the phone with my brother?"

"You missed his ass. I was on the phone with him and Natalie until Dante had to hang up the phone."

"He must got a cell phone in there with him."

"Girl, yes! He got some bitch in there doing shit for his ass."

"That sounds like Dante," Vanessa said, laughing lightly. "I ain't see a woman yet that can tell my brother no."

"That's his problem now," Alinna said with a slight attitude. "Anyways, I want you to bring A.J. over to the house on Monday morning. Dante wants me to pick up Mya from Angela's house and bring both D.J. and Mya up to the jail to see him. You can bring A.J. over so the kids can spend some time together."

"I know I'm going with ya'll to see Dante too, right?" Vanessa asked, sucking her teeth.

"Hold on, girl!" Alinna told Vanessa as she looked at her cell phone after feeling it vibrate inside her hand. It was a text from Dre explaining that he and Tony T had taken care of Sergeant Banks, Detective Fuller, and Fuller's wife.

"Vanessa," Alinna said into the phone.

"Mmm-huh!"

"Girl, what you doing?"

"Girl, your nephew's bad ass just texted me asking where I'm at, like he my mom or something."

"D.J. did something like that to me earlier," Alinna laughed.

"So what's been up with Dante and his case?" Vanessa asked, changing the subject.

"Vanessa, I wish I knew," Alinna told her girl, only to get into the whole story on what was going on with Dante and what they just found out so far about Monica and the deal she made with Sergeant Banks.

* * *

Rob dug out his ringing cell phone from his pocket just as he was finishing up a business deal with one of his regulars and two new customers that his regular had brought.

Rob walked back out to his Impala SS and answered, "Yo! Who this?"

"What's up, nigga? This ya nigga Fish Man."

"Oh shit!" Rob said, smiling as he climbed inside the Impala. "Nigga, where the fuck you been at?"

"I been handling some business," Fish Man told Rob but then asked, "What's up? You still doing ya thing out there in Miami? I'm trying to make my way back out that way again."

"Shit! I'm glad you hit me up. Shit done got sweet since this nigga Dante done got locked up. Them crackers done rammed down on his ass, and Alinna just went MIA on the street."

"Hold up!" Fish Man said. "You say this bitch nigga Dante locked up?"

"Hell yeah!" Rob said. "You ain't heard about that shit? That shit been all over the news . . . but fuck that. I got a little something I've been into, and since you called, why don't you come back out this way. We can do a little something together. What's up?"

"Hell! Fuck yeah! Let me get shit right, then I'ma get back there like yesterday, my nigga."

"That's what's up. Hit me when you touch down, and we can hook up," Rob said, hanging up the phone and still smiling.

*   *   *

"Fish, what's up, my nigga?" Russell asked as he walked into the hotel room that he and Fish Man were renting out together.

Losing his train of thought when he heard his boy Russell, Fish Man shifted his attention to homeboy and said,

"Yo! Go tell them niggas Brian, Sean, and Lloyd we leaving in the morning."

"Where we going?"

"Miami, nigga!" Fish Man said, standing up from where he was seated at the foot of his bed, before walking into the bathroom.

Fish Man shut the bathroom door behind him and turned on the water in the sink. He sat down on the toilet. Playing back over in his head what Rob had just told him about Dante being locked up and Alinna disappearing, Fish Man slowly began smiling as thoughts began forming in his head about ideas he came up with in the past.

9

Climbing out of the Phantom in front of the hotel in which Natalie was staying, Alinna was walking in the middle of her security team, with James right beside her. They entered the hotel and were on the elevator a moment later riding up to the penthouse.

Following James off the elevator once they reached the top floor, Alinna paid no attention to the security that was crowded inside the short hallway as she continued following behind James up to the front door of Natalie's penthouse. James knocked on the door.

"What's up, James?" Gomez said, but nodded to Alinna after answering the penthouse door. "Natalie is packing her things."

Alinna pushed past both James and Gomez as she entered the penthouse, leaving both bodyguards at the front door. She found Natalie talking on her cell phone in the den, with her bags.

"Mother, I'll call you back. Alinna's here!" she said, speaking into her cell phone. She hung up, looked at Alinna, and softly said, "I'm sorry for calling you so early."

"Don't apologize. You're a part of the family, Natalie," Alinna told her just as both James and Gomez entered the den. "Let's get her things out to the truck."

Turning back to Natalie and motioning for her to follow, Alinna started from the den and headed toward the sitting room while James and Gomez took care of Natalie's bags.

"Alinna, are you sure you're okay with me staying with you, now that my father . . . Dominic . . . has disowned me?" Natalie asked as she sat down beside Alinna inside of the sitting room.

"Natalie . . . listen. I respect the decision you made to stay here and support Dante while he's in jail, and it's clear that you love him. Truthfully, I felt some type of way about the love Dante so clearly has for you. But after spending time with you, I actually like you a lot more than I thought I would. Most of all, you're carrying Dante's baby. So I'm sure about this decision, and anyways, we're supposed to be moving into the new house this afternoon, so everything works out," Alinna explained.

"Alinna . . . ," James interrupted, drawing both Alinna and Natalie's attention. "The bags were sent down to the truck."

Nodding in response to James, Alinna looked back toward Natalie and asked, "You ready to go?"

Nodding her head as she slowly stood, Natalie followed Alinna to the front door. As she left the penthouse, she passed Gomez, who offered a small smile.

They took the elevator down to the first floor where they met more of Alinna's security team, along with some security team that Dominic had left behind for Natalie's protection. Both women followed their bodyguards out of the hotel while guests in the hotel's crowded lobby stared as the group left.

Natalie saw the two metallic-black GMC Yukon Denali SUVs and the two black BMW M3s that were parked in front of the hotel behind Alinna's Phantom. She climbed inside the Phantom behind Alinna. Gomez climbed up front with the driver, while James climbed in back with her and Alinna.

"James," Alinna started, getting his attention. "Have the bags sent to the penthouse. I need to pick up Mya from her mother's house."

Pulling her phone from her bag, Alinna started to call Angela's number, when her cell phone started to ring inside of her hand.

Seeing that it was Greg Wilson calling, Alinna answered the call: "Hello."

"Mrs. Blackwell, this is—"

"I already know who's calling," Alinna told the investigator, interrupting him. "What do you have for me, Greg?"

"Well, first I've got an address location for Agent Young. He lives alone," Wilson told Alinna. He then explained further: "Also, as of last month, right after Mr. Blackwell's arrest, Agent Martin resigned from the DEA She no longer has an address of residence in Miami. Agent Martin may not even be in Florida anymore."

"Wait. You said Monica left Florida?" Alinna asked. "So basically what you're telling me is that this bit . . . is that Monica just upped and disappeared, and now nobody knows where she at?"

"I've done a check with friends of Agent Martin, and I've even contacted a friend of mine with the DEA and found nothing but an old address to a younger sister of Agent Martin. I'm looking into locating the sister now."

Quiet for a few moments, thinking about a few things that just came to her, Alinna finally spoke up and said, "Find out where the sister is, Greg. I've got an extra $10,000 if you can find me that information soon."

"What about Agent Young?" Greg Wilson asked her.

"Give me the address and everything you got on Paul," Alinna told the investigator, writing down what he passed along to her. She then hung up and called Dre right away.

"Yeah. Who this?"

"Dre, this Alinna. You ready to put in some more work?"

"No doubt! What's up, Alinna?"

Alinna explained to Dre what she needed him and Tony T to handle for her. She then gave him the address that Greg Wilson found. She began to say more, when Dre interrupted,

"Yo, Alinna! I'ma have to take this nigga Dread with me. Tony T and Harmony left town this morning."

"I'm guessing when you say Dread, you mean Wesley, right?" Alinna asked, but then continued before Dre could respond. "And where did Harmony and Tony T go to?"

"North Carolina," Dre answered. "Harmony wanted to go see about her mom and little sister. Tony T said they'll be back in three days, though."

"Alright," Alinna replied, deciding to call Harmony later when she had time. "Go ahead and take Wesley with you. As a matter of fact, I want you to take Maxine, one of the twins, with you as well. Also, tell Wesley that I don't want Young's body found after you are all done."

"What if homeboy don't know nothing?" Dre asked her. "What do you want us to do then?"

"He knows something, Dre. Tell Maxine to do whatever she has to, to find out anything Young knows, alright?" Alinna told Dre, hanging up the phone right afterward.

"You're a little like Dante," Natalie told Alinna as Alinna was dialing another number on her cell phone, after watching her whole phone conversation with Dre.

"You know . . . ," Alinna started, looking over at Natalie as she was listening to the line ringing as she called Angela's phone. "I thought the same thing about you just yesterday."

* * *

Pulling up in front of Angela's house ten minutes after hanging up with her, Alinna climbed from her Phantom behind James and Natalie just as Angela stepped outside onto the porch.

"I'm pretty sure I was clear when I said that my daughter wasn't going anywhere with you," Angela said as Alinna and her friends walked up her walkway. She nodded out to the street where two Benz trucks were parked and suit-wearing men stood waiting. "You need to get your people out of the streets. You do not own this neighborhood."

"Angela, let's not go through this," Alinna told her as she and both Natalie and James stopped in front of the porch and stared. "I told you what Dante says he wants. You know how—"

"I can care less what the hell Dante wants!" Angela yelled, cutting off Alinna. "Dante's ass needs to be worried about the death sentence they about to give his ass."

"Angela . . . Everything okay?"

Looking to her right just as Geno walked up beside her, Angela answered in Spanish, "Geno, I'm fine. This is just the Alinna bitch I told you about."

"Alinna, huh?" Geno said, speaking in English as he looked over toward her.

Ignoring the whole bitch comment, Alinna looked from Angela to Geno. Recognizing the name from Dante, who had explained that Geno was Angela's brother, Alinna said, "So you're Angela's brother, huh?"

Laughing at hearing Alinna's question, Angela said, "I see Dante isn't as smart as I once thought he was. I told Dante Geno was my brother, when, in fact, he's my husband."

Slowly smiling after hearing Angela's confession, Alinna shifted her eyes over toward Geno, seeing him smirking and staring at her, unaware that Angela just signed his death sentence by admitting she lied to Dante about who he really was.

"Alinna, let's just leave, and we can let Dante know what Angela's decision is," Natalie spoke up.

Alinna looked back at Angela, only to hear her ask, "And who the hell are you?"

73

"Allow me to introduce Dante's baby's mother, Natalie Saldana," Alinna replied, smiling as she stood watching the change in Angela's facial expression.

As Alinna turned and walked away, leaving Angela staring angrily at them, she waited until the three of them were back inside the Phantom and said, "Dante is going to be pissed off once I tell him that Angela refused to let Mya come with us."

"Why are you smiling then?" Natalie asked, looking at James, who was now talking to Gomez up front, back to Alinna. "If Dante's going to be upset, what's good about that?"

"I'm not smiling because of that, Natalie. I'm smiling because I'm thinking about what Dante is gonna do once I tell him that Angela lied to him about having Mya around her supposed brother, who is, in fact, her husband."

"Alinna," James said, drawing both Alinna's and Natalie's attention to him. "I've got an idea that may just get Dante out of jail."

"How?" Both Alinna and Natalie asked.

* * *

Calling Rob as soon as he and his team reached the hotel out in Miami Lakes, Fish Man smiled once Rob answered on the start of the third ring. "Yo! What's up?"

"What's up, nigga? This Fish Man?"

"Oh shit! My nigga, where you at?"

"I'm out here in Miami Lakes," Fish Man told Rob. "What's up, though? We hooking up or what?"

"Hell yeah, my nigga!" Rob said, sounding hyped and happy to hear from his boy, Fish Man. "I'm with my lady right now, but let me drop her off real quick, and then we can meet up then. Where at out in Miami Lakes you at?"

Giving Rob the location of the hotel where he was staying, Fish Man hung up with Rob and then walked into the hotel room which he was splitting with Russell, only to be hit in the face by strong weed smoke.

"What's up, Fish?" Russell asked, handing over the blunt he was smoking. "What ya homeboy talking about?"

"He coming through in a little while," Fish Man answered, taking a pull from the blunt. "Go get them other fools. We got some shit to discuss before my dude gets here."

* * *

Back inside the penthouse, Alinna was sitting in the den with Vanessa and Amber while Natalie got herself together inside the extra bedroom.

Seeing that Greg Wilson was calling on her phone, Alinna answered the call and said, "Tell me you've got something on Monica, Greg."

"Actually, I've come up with the same thing as before, but something isn't right, Mrs. Blackwell."

"What do you mean?"

"I've spoken with a few people I know down at the police department, and I've heard a few things about Angela, who's the captain down at the department. It seems like her name is on everyone's lips, but nobody knows what's going on. I do know that the chief of police is supposed to be calling a meeting with Captain Angela Perez and the agent who was in charge of the investigation against Mr. Blackwell."

"Wait a minute! Why the hell is the DEA and the chief of police meeting with Angela when Dante's already locked up?"

"That's what I'm checking into now," the investigator told Alinna. "Also, I've contacted a friend and came up with an address for Agent Martin's sister. It's a Tampa address inside of the Temple Terrace area."

"Give me the address," Alinna told Wilson as she grabbed for a pen and something to write on. After copying down the address, she continued, "Greg, listen . . . find out everything you can about Angela. Something's not right with her."

"I'll see what I can come up with," he told Alinna, hanging up the phone afterward.

"Alinna, what happen?" Vanessa asked as Alinna was setting down her cell phone on top of the coffee table.

"Something's not right, Vanessa!" Alinna told her girl, shaking her head slowly with a faraway look on her face. "That was Greg Wilson, the investigator that works for us. He just told me something about Angela and Monica that doesn't sit well with me."

"What he say?" Amber asked just as Natalie entered the den.

Asking Natalie to sit down, Alinna went into the whole conversation she just had with Greg Wilson, starting with Monica's disappearance and then about the up-and-coming meeting that was to happen between Angela and both the chief of police and the DEA agent in charge of Dante's case.

"It sounds like both Monica and Dante's supposed baby mama got something going on together. What you think, A?" Amber asked Alinna, staring at her girl with a questioning expression on her face.

Shaking her head, unable to answer Amber's question, Alinna sat in deep thought, trying to put everything together that Greg Wilson had explained to her. She lost her train of thought when her cell phone rang from the coffee table.

Picking up the iPhone and seeing that it was Dre calling, Alinna answered: "Hello."

"We took care of that homeboy," Dre told Alinna. "We really ain't get nothing from homeboy but two addresses. One's to a sister of ya girl you looking for, and some cabin ya girl and her husband own out in Georgia."

"Alright. Come back to the penthouse. I've got something I wanna tell the rest of the family."

"We on our way."

Alinna hung up the phone, looked over at Vanessa, and said, "Dre and them on their way back. They took care of Monica's partner, Agent Paul Young. But Dre say that Paul gave up two addresses: one to Monica's sister and another to some cabin out in Georgia that Monica and Alex owned."

"We're going out to this cabin, right?" Natalie asked, drawing Alinna's and the others' attention to her.

"We're definitely going," Alinna answered, locking eyes with Natalie.

*　　*　　*

Hanging up the phone with Rob, who called to say he was outside in the parking lot of the hotel, Fish Man told his team that Rob was on his way up to the room as he was headed to the bathroom to take a piss.

Finishing up inside the bathroom, Fish Man walked out to see Rob leaned up against the wall near the door laughing and smoking a blunt with the others. "What's up, nigga?"

"Nigga, you wash ya hands?" Rob asked jokingly, causing the others to laugh as he pushed Fish Man's hands out of the way from in front of him.

"Whatever, nigga!" Fish Man said, turning around, walking to the bed, and sitting down at the foot of the bed. "So what's up, my dude? What's this surprise you say you got for me, and when this bitch nigga Dante went in?"

"First, this clown-ass nigga Dante let them crackers run down on his ass up in the club on Alinna's birthday. That shit been all over the TV for almost two months now. This crazy-ass nigga killed a DEA agent and the captain on the MDPD," Rob explained.

"What about Alinna?" Fish Man asked.

"Shit! Don't nobody really know what's up with shorty. She still around 'cause muthafuckers be seeing that Rolls Royce Phantom the nigga Dante got her for her birthday. But as far as the game go, I think shorty done left the shit alone since Dante gone," Rob explained. He then gave Fish Man a big smile and continued, "And that brings me to the surprise I've got for you. The streets is wide the fuck open, and if you ready, we about to take over Miami like nobody ever have. What's up?"

"How you plan on doing that?" Brian spoke up.

"I've got this connect I'm fucking without in Fort Lauderdale, but homeboy got that real shit, and he ain't working with nothing but coke and heroin."

"What dude name is?" Fish Man asked. "We was just out in Fort Lauderdale before we got here."

"Some young nigga named Kyree," Rob answered, smiling at Fish Man.

"Naw, I ain't never heard of dude. But we did hear about some young nigga that open up some spot out in Devin Hunt area over in them cream and brown apartments," Fish Man explained.

"That's my nigga!" Rob said, nodding his head. "That's the nigga, Kyree. Dude got a team out there with his ass, and shit is for real with homeboy. But he's talking right on the prices, though."

Slowing nodding his head to what Rob was explaining but thinking of other plans that weren't anywhere close to what Rob was talking about, Fish Man slowly smiled and said, "A'ight, my dude. I'm all in. So let's talk numbers now."

10

Angela left Mya at home with her husband and sitter as she drove away from her house. She called her assistant's desk and pulled up in front of a McDonald's. The phone picked up on the other end as her assistant said, "Captain Perez's desk. This is Joanna, Captain Perez's assistant. How can I help you?"

"Joanna, it's Angela . . ."

"Oh my God, Angela," Joanna cried into the phone, cutting her off. "I tried to call you a few minutes ago. Chief Johnson and Agent Murphy are here waiting for you. They've been here for a little over twenty minutes."

"You say the chief and Agent Murphy?" Angela asked, balling up her face. "You talking about Agent Murphy with the DEA?"

"Yes. It's the same DEA agent that was helping with the Dante Blackwell case."

"What do they want?"

"There's been talk of a meeting, but I haven't been told anything yet."

Angela was quiet as she pulled her car forward. There were still four cars ahead of her at the drive-thru. She finally spoke up: "Okay, Joanna. If the chief asks if I called in, let him know I said I'll be in, in about fifteen minutes, but don't mention anything we discussed."

"Of course, Angela."

Hanging up with her assistant with an odd feeling in her gut, Angela sat in thought for a few minutes wondering why her boss and the agent in charge of the Dante case for the DEA would be in her office waiting for her.

The horn blaring behind her broke her train of thought. Angela cut her eyes over to the rearview mirror and saw a black Escalade behind her. She then pulled up in front of the order speaker to order breakfast.

After ordering, Angela pulled up behind the car in front of her at the pay window. She then picked up her cell phone and dialed her lawyer's number, still having an odd feeling about what was going on at her office.

* * *

Alinna smiled at seeing Dante appear in front of the visitation window as she, Natalie, Vanessa, and D.J. sat waiting until he and the rest of the inmates were allowed inside the contact visitation area. She remained sitting when Dante finally walked inside the room, while D.J. took off toward his father. Natalie and Vanessa stood there smiling.

The women all watched as Dante carried D.J. and walked toward them. Alinna waited while he hugged an excited Vanessa and then gave a hug and kiss to Natalie.

"What's up, shorty?" Dante said after releasing Natalie and looking at Alinna and meeting her eyes.

Alinna slowly stood up and walked up to Dante as he put down D.J. She reached up and wrapped her arms around his neck. She could feel his arms wrap around her waist as he lifted her up in the air, and he leaned in to kiss her lips.

"I love you!" Dante told her after he and Alinna ended their kiss while still holding each other.

"I love you too, Dante," Alinna told him, kissing him again before he sat her back onto her feet, releasing her.

Alinna sat down across from Dante, who sat on the same side where the other inmates sat. She couldn't help but smile as Dante picked up D.J. and set him on his lap.

"So how you holding up, big bruh?" Vanessa asked, speaking up first, smiling across at Dante.

"I'm doing what I do. Where my brother and nephew at? Why they ain't come with you?"

"Dre handling some business, and your nephew with Harmony and Tony T out of town."

Nodding his head in response, Dante shifted his eyes over to a smiling Natalie, meeting her eyes: "What's up, beautiful?"

"I love you, Dante!" Natalie cried as tears began running down her face even though she was still smiling at him.

"I love you too, Natalie," Dante told her, winking his eye at her, which caused Natalie to lightly laugh.

"Mother told me to tell you that she misses and loves you and that that she's sorry she couldn't see you before she left with Dominic."

"She was down here?"

"Yes, but Dominic came and took her back home."

"Why didn't you go back also?"

"Because you're still locked inside this place, and I no longer have a home to go back to."

"What the fuck!"

"She's living with us now, Dante," Alinna spoke up, seeing the look that appeared on his face.

"What happen?" Dante asked, staring hard and straight at Alinna.

"It's not important!" Alinna told him. "If you're wondering why Mya isn't here, Angela wouldn't let her come with us."

"I figured that when I didn't see her here when I walked in," Dante explained. "What she say when you told her what I said?"

"She said fuck you, Dante!" Natalie replied, telling Dante. "She said that she didn't give a fuck what you wanted and that you should be more concerned about the death sentence they're trying to give you."

Slowly nodding his head after listening to what Natalie just told him, Dante shifted his eyes back to Alinna as she asked, "Did you know that Angela is married?"

Seeing the look on his face, Alinna continued, "You remember her brother, Geno, who you met when you went over to see Mya? Well, Angela admitted that she lied about Geno being her brother. He's actually her husband."

"So what's up with the case, Alinna?" Dante asked, speaking through tight lips.

Seeing the anger building on his face, Alinna still went ahead and told him everything she now knew about what was going on with his case, from the issue with Monica to what was happening with Angela and her meeting with the chief of police and the DEA.

"Find Monica!" Dante said as soon as Alinna finished talking. "Put somebody on Angela and keep a watch on her ass, Alinna. But I want you to do whatever you have to do, and get me the fuck out of here!"

"I'm already on it, Dante," she told him, staring back as they held each other's stare.

*   *   *

Seated behind her desk after her meeting with the chief of police and Agent Murphy, Angela was deep in thought about what was said inside the meeting and all the questions that were asked concerning the disappearance of Sergeant Aaron Banks and Detective Howard Fuller.

Digging out her cell phone from her bag, Angela dialed the number she had for Agent Monica Martin, only to hear that the number was no longer in service.

"What in the . . . !" Angela started, but then quickly dialed the number to DEA headquarters.

Angela finally reached and spoke with someone at the front office of the DEA. She found out that Monica was not only not in at the office, but that she had also resigned from the agency. Angela asked the woman she was speaking with for a number to contact Agent Monica Martin, only to find out that the agency didn't have contact info for the resigned agent.

"What the fuck is going on?" Angela said out loud to herself after hanging up the phone with the DEA agency.

The odd feeling she was having now turned into a strong feeling of worry. Angela was just about to make another call when her desk phone rang and her assistant, Joanna, rushed into the office.

"That's the chief calling you," she warned her boss.

"Captain Perez," Angela answered the phone, staring straight at Joanna.

"Angela . . . it's Johnson. You got a minute?"

"Sure, Chief. What's up?"

"I just got a call from Agent Murphy. It looks like Agent Paul Young, who was a part of the investigation, has now also turned up missing. He was supposed to show up for work today and never did. Also, no one's been able to contact him. When another agent was sent over to his house, he wasn't there, but his car was parked inside of the yard."

"What time did this agent go by to see if Agent Young was home?"

"This morning."

"What about his family? Has anyone called or gone by his family's house to speak with them?"

"Agent Young isn't from Florida, and the only family he has live in Baton Rouge, Louisiana."

Going into her own thoughts while Chief Johnson continued talking, Angela really didn't pay much attention to what was being said anymore. She caught the ending of

Chief Johnson's letting her know that he would contact her later. She then hung up the phone and fell back into her desk chair.

"What's going on, Angela?" Joanna asked her boss after Angela hung up.

"I wish I knew," Angela answered. She had a plan to get to the bottom of whatever was happening—and soon.

* * *

"Here goes my nigga now!" Rob said, nodding to Kyree as homeboy came walking out of the trap house talking on his cell phone.

Fish Man stared out the back of his Escalade as he, Rob, Russell, Sean, and Brian sat out in front of the trap house. Fish Man sat watching the young dude as he was walking far away from the front gate. Noticing the four other guys not very far from the young dude, he followed Rob from the Escalade and walked over to the front gate.

"What's up, Rob?" Kyree said as he slid his cell phone into his pocket. He then nodded over to Fish Man and said, "This ya man you was telling me about?"

"Yo, Kyree. This my nigga, Fish Man," Rob introduced the two.

Kyree talked with Rob's homeboy, Fish Man, a few minutes to get a feel for him. He then finally got to more important matters and asked, "So what's up, playboy? What you and this nigga Rob talking about copping?"

"My dude Rob already done gave me ya prices, so you think you can fuck with three of them things?" Fish Man asked, staring into Kyree's eyes.

Doing some quick math in his head, Kyree slowly nodded his heading and said, "I'ma fuck with you on the three. You got that $7,500 now, or you need some time?"

"You got that work now, or do YOU need some time?" Fish Man responded while holding Kyree's eye contact.

Slowly smiling, Kyree said, "Get up with me tomorrow at 12:00. I'ma have that ready for you."

"That'll work," Fish Man said as he and Kyree dapped.

* * *

"When we leaving to handle this with the cabin out in Georgia, Alinna?" Vanessa asked as she, Alinna, Natalie, and D.J. drove away from the county jail after finishing their contact visit with Dante.

"Call Tony T and Harmony, and see if they back yet," Alinna told Vanessa while staring out the back window of her Phantom and thinking about the look on Dante's face when he told her to do whatever she had to in order to get him out of jail.

Pulling out her cell phone, Alinna called Dre's number.

"Who this?"

"Dre, this Alinna. Where are you?"

"We just got back to the penthouse from grabbing something to eat. Why? What's up now?"

"We changing up plans!" Alinna told Dre. She then explained that he and Wesley were going out to see Monica's sister and pick up her and her husband, and then contact her once they had them.

Alinna finished up her phone call with Dre and explained everything she needed him to do. She then hung up the phone, only to look over at Vanessa after hearing her call out to her and hold out her cell phone for Alinna.

"It's Tony T," Vanessa told Alinna, releasing the cell phone.

"Tony T. Where you at?" Alinna spoke into the phone.

"Me and Harmony about to take A.J. to get something to eat. Why? What's up?"

"Meet me at the penthouse after you and Harmony finish. We've got some stuff to handle."

"We'll be there in a few minutes," Tony T replied. "Hold up, though. Harmony wants to talk to you."

Waiting until Harmony got on the phone, Alinna barely heard everything Harmony was telling her. But she caught a few things Harmony mentioned about something her mother had sent her.

After hanging up the phone with Harmony, Alinna looked at Natalie and heard her ask, "You're planning on killing everybody on this case in order for Dante to walk free, aren't you?"

Staring back at Natalie a moment, Alinna said, "If there are no witnesses, then what can they say about Dante?"

Slowly nodding her head in understanding, Natalie turned her attention out the window, feeling a small smile pulling at her lips.

* * *

When they arrived back at the penthouse, Dre, Wesley, and Maxine were already there. Maxine walked straight up to James and pulled him away from Gomez. Alinna ignored the two while leading the others into the den as D.J. rushed off to the back of the penthouse.

"So what's the play, Alinna?" Dre asked as he leaned back into the couch while Vanessa sat on his lap.

"We're getting Dante out of jail before they can get him sent to prison," Alinna told the group. "He goes before the judge tomorrow at noon."

"How you plan on getting Dante out?" Maxine asked as she stood next to James at the entrance to the den.

"Think about it. If the courts don't have no witnesses, who can testify against him?" Alinna asked, looking at each of the faces inside the room with her. "The state really doesn't have anything to hold Dante, and the federal court really don't have anything either, or Dante would already be locked up inside of a federal jail waiting to see a federal judge. The only thing that's holding Dante where he is, is whoever this person is that's working with the courts."

"So again . . . ," Maxine said, speaking up, "How are you planning on getting Dante out? We don't know who this person is that's telling."

"I think I have an idea who it may be," Alinna said with a faraway look on her face. But she quickly focused back on what she was talking about. "This is what we're going to do. First, I want to find Monica's sister, and we're going to hold onto her until we find out exactly where Monica is. As for the DEA agent in charge of Dante's case, he's going to be taken care of as well. I also want the state attorney on this case to be handled, too."

"What about the judge?" Tony T asked, drawing everyone's attention to him and Harmony as they stood with Maxine, James, and Natalie's bodyguard, Gomez, at the entrance.

Nodding her head slowly as Vanessa walked over to Harmony and took her sleeping son, A.J., Alinna agreed with Tony T and said, "He's a part of the case as well, so the judge gets handled as well."

"So basically everybody dies so my brother comes home. I'm with it!" Dre said, smiling.

"Me got one question!" Wesley spoke up from beside Amber. "When do we start the blood clot killing? Me want me brethren back home."

Looking to Dre, Alinna asked, "Dre, what time you and Wesley leaving for Tampa?"

"Now!" Dre answered, lightly slapping Vanessa on the ass for her to get back up from his lap. He nodded to Wesley but then looked over at Alinna and said, "Write down the address where we're headed in Tampa."

While writing down the address for Dre, Alinna said to Tony T and Vanessa, "I want the two of you to come with me, Natalie, James, and Gomez. Harmony and Amber, I want ya'll to keep a watch on Angela while I'm gone. Maxine and Keisha will be with the two of you for backup, just in case. I'll also leave you some of our men as extra backup if ya'll need it."

"Why are we watching Angela?" Amber asked.

"Dante wants her watched, and I agree with him now," Alinna answered while handing Dre the paper on which she had been writing the address.

"When are we leaving?" Tony T asked Alinna, pulling out his vibrating cell phone and glancing down at the phone's screen.

"We're leaving tonight," Alinna answered, standing up from the sofa, only to pause as Vanessa said, "Alinna, you do remember we're supposed to have moved into the new house today, right?"

"Shit!" Alinna exclaimed, completely forgetting about the new house. "Alright, Vanessa. You take care of things with the house. Get some moving people to help you, but then make sure you take care of what I asked concerning Angela."

Leaving the den and the family, Alinna went to find Rose, the housekeeper, to explain that she was leaving town for a few days.

11

Angela walked out to her car, leaving the station during her lunch break, when her cell phone started ringing. She dug out both the phone and her car keys, just as she was walking around to the driver's side of her car.

She unlocked the door and then climbed inside. Angela then answered the phone without first checking the caller ID: "Captain Perez."

Angela heard the prompts from a collect call from Dante at the county jail, so she hung up and tossed the phone over onto the passenger seat with her bag. She cranked up the car, throwing it in reverse, and backed out of the parking lot just as her cell phone went off again.

She snatched up the phone, looked at the caller ID, and saw an unlisted name and number. Angela sent the call to voicemail, already knowing it was Dante calling back again.

She then dropped the phone into her lap and pulled up to a stoplight. She instantly began thinking about the disappearances of Monica and Agent Paul Young, as well as both Detective Fuller and Sergeant Banks.

Hearing the horns behind her begin to honk took her out of her thoughts, and Angela noticed that the light was now green. She pulled off, still a bit confused on what the hell was going on. She was really beginning to worry.

"What the hell!" Angela said, snatching up her ringing phone from her lap and glancing at the screen to see the unlisted name and number. She answered, "Hello?"

"You forgetting how to answer a phone now, huh?"

Hearing Dante's voice and not the automated operator, Angela felt her heart pick up speed and beat hard against her chest. She finally spoke, "Da . . . Dante. How are you calling me?"

"I got your message, Angela," Dante told her, ignoring her question. "So since you feel how you do and since you're refusing to let Mya come see me as I requested, I'll deal with things my way. Tell me something, though, Angela. Why is it that the DEA handed over the case to your people and not handle it themselves?"

"W . . . What are you talking about, Dante?" Angela asked, surprised at what he was asking her.

"I see you've taken up playing games now!" he told her. "Don't worry about it, Angela. As I said before, I'll handle things my way. Yeah! Don't disappear any time soon. I'll see you real soon."

Hearing Dante hang up the phone, Angela had to pull over to the side of the road, feeling her hands shaking too hard. She sat inside her car playing back in her head his words before he had hung up the phone: "Don't disappear any time soon. I'll see you soon!"

Angela quickly called her husband's phone to tell him that she was on her way home, only to hear her husband's voicemail pick up. Angela hung up the phone and then called the house phone, only for that phone to ring and ring over and over.

"Oh God!" Angela cried in a panic, dropping her phone into her lap as she quickly switched her car into drive, pulling off back into the intersection, ignoring the horns blowing behind her.

Speeding and running red lights, Angela swung down her street ten minutes later, slamming on the brakes in front of her house. She hopped from the car and rushed around, noticing both her husband and sitter's cars parked in the driveway.

Angela unlocked the front door and opened it. She rushed inside the house and yelled out her husband's and sitter's names. She ran through each room inside the house, only to find each one of them empty. Angela then ended up standing in the middle of the floor inside the den, staring around in a state of confusion and fear.

Angela was startled when she heard the house phone ring. She rushed into the kitchen and snatched up the phone from the base. "Hello! Geno!"

"So that's who you're expecting, is it?"

Hearing Dante's voice again, she remained quiet a moment. Angela then asked, "Dante, where the hell are my brother and my daughter?"

"Both your husband and my daughter are safe," Dante told her, but then added, "Like I said beginning back from the first phone call, don't disappear any time soon. I'll be in contact real soon."

Hearing him hang up again, Angela felt her strength leave her. She fell back against the counter as tears of fear and frustration ran down her face.

Getting control of herself, she dialed the number out to the jail where Dante was supposed to be getting connected with booking. However, she found out that he was, in fact, still locked up. She thanked the woman on the phone and then turned and hung up her house phone.

Noticing the yellow sticky note on top of the counter, Angela picked it up and read it out loud: "Contact DEA or the MDPD and you'll never see your husband alive again, and Mya will never see her mother again. We'll be in touch."

"Son of a bitch!" Angela yelled, balling up the note and tossing it onto the counter in anger.

* * *

"Hello!"

"What's up, shorty? Where you at?"

"Heading to Georgia. What's up, Dante?"

"I holla'ed at Amber and Vanessa. They took care of something for me."

Alinna started to ask Dante what he was talking about but changed her mind, figuring he would tell her if he wanted her to know, so she instead said, "I spoke with Mr. Goldmen and Mr. Sutter. The shipment will be here or back in Miami tomorrow. I've got Vanessa and Kyree taking care of the pickup tomorrow."

"Who the hell is Kyree?"

"Vanessa brought him to the family. So far, he's doing good business."

"You say Vanessa brought him in?"

"Yes, Dante."

"Alright. Where Natalie at?"

"Hold on," Alinna told Dante as she passed the cell phone back to Natalie.

"Hello."

"What's up, beautiful? You alright?"

"Yes, Dante," Natalie answered with a smile. "How are you doing?"

"I'm good. I just wanted to check up on you. Let me talk to Gomez real quick."

"I love you!" Natalie told him as she did as she was told, handing over the cell phone to Gomez and explaining to the bodyguard that it was Dante on the phone.

"Dante . . . my friend."

"Gomez. What's up, big man?" Dante said, but continued before Gomez could respond. "Listen, Gomez. I'm holding you responsible for Natalie and my seed's safety. Anything happens to them—"

"Relax, Dante," Gomez told him, cutting off Dante. "I will give my life for Natalie and the baby. You have nothing to worry about. I promise my life to you that she will be safe."

"I'ma hold you to that promise, Gomez," Dante told the big man in all seriousness. "Put Alinna back on the phone."

"Yes, Dante," Alinna said into the phone after taking the cell phone from Gomez.

"Where's James?"

"He's up front with Gomez driving. You wanna talk to him?"

"I'm good," Dante answered. "I know James handling his business. I really just wanted to hear your voice."

"I love you too, Dante," Alinna told him, smiling.

Hanging up with Dante after a few more minutes and still smiling, Alinna looked over at Natalie and said, "We've really got to get him out of jail, Natalie."

"I was just thinking the same exact thing, Alinna. We really need to," Natalie replied, smiling back at Alinna.

* * *

"Agent Murphy, sir!"

Looking up from the papers he was reading over at his desk, and seeing his assistant at his office door, Agent Murphy waved the assistant inside the office and said, "What is it, Rachel?"

"Sir, I just put the call you've been waiting for through to your phone," the assistant told Murphy, nodding toward the desk phone.

Instantly catching on to who was holding on his phone, Agent Murphy snatched up the desk phone headset. He then hit the blinking red light on the phone and asked, "Martin, you there?"

"Yeah, Victor," Monica Martin answered. "I got your message. What's this about Paul disappearing?"

"I sent a team over to Agent Young's house after he didn't show up this morning and wasn't answering his phone. His car was in the driveway, but when the agents got into the house, Agent Young wasn't there."

"Has anyone called his personal cell phone yet?"

"I called it myself," Agent Murphy answered, but then said, "The thing is that the two detectives we gave the arrest to for Dante Blackwell . . . they're also now missing as well. Even Detective Howard Fuller's wife is missing, Martin."

"Where is Blackwell? Is he still in jail?"

"Of course."

Quiet for a few moments thinking, Monica finally spoke up: "What about Angela? Where is she? Have you kept a tail on her like we agreed?"

"Relax, Martin," Agent Murphy told her. "We've been keeping a close eye on Captain Perez. We've even caught her visiting Blackwell, but she couldn't get inside because of a visit from a Natalie Saldana that Blackwell accepted."

"Wait a minute! You said Natalie Saldana . . . right, Victor?" Monica asked. "Where have we heard the name Saldana before?"

"What do you—?"

"Come on, Victor!" Monica said, cutting off Agent Murphy. "Dominic Saldana . . . out in Phoenix."

"You mean the same Dominican drug lord out in Phoenix? What the hell does Blackwell got with Dominic Saldana's daughter? How the hell does he even know her?" Agent Murphy asked, sounding both surprised and shocked.

"I'll admit, Victor . . . Dante is extremely handsome, so I can see how Dominic's daughter would be interested in him. But knowing what Dante is capable of and how deadly and ruthless he can be, that easily explains Dominic's interest in Dante," Monica replied. "Victor . . . you need to put a trail on Alinna Rodriguez and talk with Chief Johnson about seeing if he can have Dante moved into a more secure jail than the Miami-Dade County Jail."

"I'll look into that," Agent Murphy replied, but then asked, "Where exactly are you at, Martin?"

"You know how to find me if you need me, Victor," Monica told her ex-boss. "I'll see you when the time comes to stand before the judge. I gotta go."

"Mart . . . !" Agent Murphy heard Monica hang up the phone, cutting him off as he was speaking. He sighed deeply as he hung up his phone, shaking his head and thinking about what he and Monica had just finished discussing.

12

Alinna made it back to Miami a few hours after leaving Georgia, where she found Monica's cabin empty and in a condition suggesting no one had stayed there for some time. She now sat inside of the courtroom, with Natalie next to her, and with James and Gomez sitting behind them. She ignored the cameras and the people staring and pointing at her.

"Alinna . . . !" Natalie cried, reaching over lightly and squeezing her hand to get her attention. She then smiled, nodded, and said, "There goes Dante."

Slowly allowing a small smile to show at seeing Dante in a silk white and gray Armani suit, Alinna met his eyes when he looked over at her, winking his eye at her.

Alinna held Dante's eyes the whole time they were in the courtroom with his attorney, Jonathan King, and his team. She caught a little of what the judge and the state attorney were saying about denying Dante a bond, as well as the state attorney asking the judge for more time. She then heard the judge grant the state attorney's request and set Dante's next court date for two weeks.

Alinna watched Dante being escorted back out of the courtroom. Catching the wink of an eye he shot her as he left, she stood from her seat, causing James, Gomez, and Natalie to stand as well as they all followed Alinna out of the room.

Alinna allowed James to lead, while Gomez followed behind the women. Alinna then pulled out her cell phone from her Dolce & Gabbana bag. She turned her iPhone back on, only to see two missed calls and a voice message from a few minutes earlier.

Seeing that both Dre and Amber had called, Alinna first checked her message before calling either of them back.

"I've got information you may want. I'll be in touch real soon," Alinna heard on her phone message. She stopped right outside of the courthouse in front of the entrance.

"James!" Natalie cried after Alinna's sudden stop. Seeing the look on her face, she asked, "Alinna, are you okay?"

"Alinna! What's up?" James asked as he quickly stopped in front of her in three steps. "What happened?"

"Listen to this," she told James, handing him her cell phone before she began walking again.

Following alongside Alinna on her right while listening to the message on her phone, James played the message again, handed the phone back to Alinna, and then asked, "You don't know who that was?"

Shaking her head in response to James's question, Alinna was deep in thought when they walked up to the Phantom and her phone rang inside her hand. She answered it as she was climbing inside the car: "Hello?"

"Did you get my message?"

Quiet for a moment and meeting James's eyes, Alinna asked, "Who the hell is this?"

"Who I am isn't important right now, but what I have to tell you is. Do you want to meet?"

"What can you tell me that's so important that I would agree to meet with you without knowing who the hell you are?"

"I know who the informant is on Dante Blackwell's case, and I know who set all this up against Dante Blackwell. Are you interested in hearing this information or not?"

"What is it you want?" Alinna asked, sighing into the phone.

"I want $5 million," the caller told Alinna.

"Only $5 million? That's all?" Alinna asked sarcastically. "I tell you what, muthafucker: I'll meet with you, and if what you have to tell me is worth it, then I'll give you the money."

"I'll be in contact," the caller told her, hanging up the phone afterward.

"Who was that, Alinna?" Natalie asked, seeing her lower the phone from her ear, only for the phone to start ringing again.

"Yeah, Dre!" Alinna answered after seeing it was him calling.

"What's up, Alinna? Where you at?"

"On the way back to the house."

"Well, we took care of that little issue out in Tampa you told us to handle, and we got it at one of Harmony's spots out in the city."

"Alright. Find out where Monica at, and if they won't talk, let Maxine and Keisha talk with 'em," Alinna told Dre. "I'll be there later."

Hanging up with Dre, Alinna then called Amber back.
"Hello."

"Amber, this Alinna. What's up? You called me earlier?"

"Alinna, you not gonna believe this shit!" Amber started, but quickly continued, "We was keeping a watch on Angela's ass like you wanted and ended up finding out something else. We weren't the only ones following her."

"Who else?" Alinna asked eagerly.

"Not really sure, but it's got to be some type of police."

"Where you at now?"

"I'm with Vanessa right now. We about to meet up with Keisha and Kyree at Vanessa's spot out in Fort Lauderdale."

"Who's watching Angela?"

"Harmony's with Maxine. They're watching Angela right now, but we're hooking back up with them later after Vanessa takes care of this business with Kyree."

"Alright. I'll call you later," Alinna told her girl, hanging up the phone, only to go right back to thinking about the caller with the information for her.

Looking at her cell phone screen, and seeing the time, Alinna wondered when Dante was planning on calling her, so she could tell him about the caller and what Amber just told her about Angela being followed.

* * *

Pulling up in front of the Fort Lauderdale trap house just as an Escalade was pulling off, Vanessa parked her truck behind a nice-looking Lexus that was parked in front.

"Vanessa . . . look!" Amber said at seeing Keisha climbing from the passenger seat of the Lexus. "Who that Keisha with?"

"I'm wondering the same thing!" Vanessa replied as she turned off the Benz truck, then climbed out and called to Keisha: "What's up, Keisha? Who's your friend?"

"It's okay, Vanessa. It's just my boyfriend, and he's about to leave now," Keisha explained.

"What's up, Vanessa?" Rob called out from the driver's window of the Lexus. After noticing her, he climbed out of his car.

"Look who it is!" Amber said, looking Rob over with a slight frown. "What you doing here, Rob?"

"What's it to you, Amber?" he said, showing a small smile while shaking his head and staring at her with a sarcastic look.

"Wait a minute! Ya'll know each other?" Keisha asked, looking from Rob to Vanessa to Amber and back to Rob again.

"Let's just say we got a little history together," Rob answered just as he was pulling out his ringing cell phone.

"What's up, Vanessa?" Kyree asked, walking out the front gate and stopping to hug Amber. He then turned to face Vanessa and said, "Everything set up inside. You brought that with you?"

"It's in the trunk," Vanessa told Kyree, handing him her truck keys before shifting her attention back over to Rob just in time to catch Keisha kissing him goodbye.

Shaking her head but saying nothing, Vanessa followed both Kyree and Amber from outside to inside the trap house to finish handling the business with Kyree.

* * *

"You plan on telling me how you know Vanessa and Amber, Rob?" Keisha asked, sounding a little jealous while staring directly into his eyes.

"We used to fuck with each other back in the days before shit kind of went sour!" he briefly explained, but then quickly asked, "What you know about He-She and Amber?"

"Who the fuck is He-She, Rob?" Keisha asked, staring at him with a balled up face.

"That's what everybody used to call Vanessa back in the day," Rob told her. "She used to be mean as fuck before she got with that nigga Dre and had that baby. Vanessa was worse than most niggas out here on these streets, and she was just as quick to knock a nigga and bust a nigga's ass in a heartbeat. That ho is Alinna's right-hand bitch."

Hearing the way Rob was talking about her team and staring at him as he was reading a text message on his phone,

Keisha decided she would question Vanessa and Alinna about Rob later on when she got the chance.

"Keisha, let me holla at you later, shorty!" Rob told her, kissing her lips and then climbing back inside his Lexus.

Standing out in front of the trap house and watching Rob as he drove off, Keisha found herself slightly hoping she didn't find anything fucked up about Rob, since she was actually starting to catch feelings for him now.

*   *   *

Climbing out of the Phantom in front of the trap house in the city run by Harmony, Alinna allowed James and Gomez to lead the way while she and Natalie followed with a team of men surrounding them. She looked around and saw that since the spot was closed, the area was deserted of its normal crowd. She only saw a few people walking the streets.

She entered the house just as Dre stood up from the brown sofa he was seated on across from Wesley, who was smoking a blunt. Alinna then wasted no time and asked, "Where are they at?"

"In the back room with Maxine," Dre answered, nodding his head toward the back of the house.

Alinna walked off and found the bedroom where Maxine was keeping Monica's family. Their muffled screams could be heard before Alinna even opened the door. As she did, two of her men shifted toward the door but relaxed when it was opened and they saw Maxine in control of the situation.

They watched as Maxine was going to work on the tall and slim brown-skinned man tied to a wooden chair, next to a darker-skinned female who was also tied and gagged to another chair. Maxine was pouring a clear liquid onto the man's bleeding scrotum, causing him to scream out in pain behind his gagged mouth. Alinna calmly called to Maxine to get her attention: "Let me talk to 'em for a moment. Pull the gag off from the woman's mouth so she can talk."

Holding the woman's eyes as Maxine moved around behind her and began untying the gag, Alinna spoke up and said, "If you scream once the gag is removed, I will have you killed."

"What's going on? Who are you?" the woman begged, staring at Alinna standing in front of her. "Why are we even here?"

"I'm going to make this simple, Nicole," Alinna started, using the woman's name and seeing the change in her expression. "I want to know where your sister, Monica, is, and understand that if you lie or waste my time, I will kill you and your husband. Again, I ask you, where is your sister?"

Staring at Alinna standing in front of her with a serious face, Nicole softly said, "What are you going to do with me and my husband if I tell you what I know?"

"We can discuss that after you've answered my questions," Alinna responded, folding her arms across her chest. "I'm waiting, Nicole."

Taking a deep breath and then slowly releasing it, Nicole looked over to her husband, who was unconscious beside her. She looked back to the women and said, "I only know that Monica is in Florida City somewhere with an old friend she used to work with at the DEA."

"What's this friend's name?" Natalie asked from beside Alinna, stepping up from where she stood with both James and Gomez against the wall next to the bedroom door.

Staring at the other Spanish woman she hadn't noticed earlier, Nicole looked back to the first woman and said, "Her name is Evelyn Owens."

"How do you contact her?" Alinna asked Nicole.

"I don't . . . Wait!" Nicole cried as Alinna held up her hand for the woman torturing her husband to stop.

"I'm listening, Nicole," Alinna said calmly. "This had better be something I want to hear."

"I can't contact Monica, but she calls me. She's supposed to call me tonight at 10:00 p.m.," Nicole explained, watching as Alinna looked back over at the two men leaning against the wall.

"It's 7:15," James told Alinna, checking his Kenneth Cole watch that she had bought for him.

Looking back at Nicole, Alinna said, "You better hope your sister calls, or I promise you I'ma have something worse than death for you and your husband."

*　*　*

Hearing her phone cranking up and ringing from the passenger seat as he was driving off from handling business, Rob snatched up the phone, saw it was Fish Man, and answered, "What's up, nigga?"

"What's up, my dude? You tried to hit me earlier today?"

"Hell yea. You not gonna believe who the fuck I ran into earlier while I was with my lady over at this nigga Kyree's spot."

"Who that, nigga?"

"This bitch Vanessa and Amber ass. Them the same hoes that was fucking with that bitch Alinna's ass."

"Fuck was they doing over there?"

"I guess they was copping work from this nigga too, but they look like they still sitting on some paper. They pulled up in a Benz truck and was looking fly as hell, too."

"Dude, you sound like a fan and shit. Fuck is wrong with you?"

"Fuck all that you talking about, nigga? I just respect them hoes when they was running shit out here. They was doing shit big for a minute."

"Fuck them hoes!" Fish Man said, sounding pissed off. "You ain't see that bitch Alinna with 'em?"

"Nigga, didn't I just say I saw Vanessa and that bitch Amber. What's up with you sweating that bitch, Alinna?"

"Ain't nobody sweating that bitch! I just owe her ass for trying to shine on me the last time I saw the bitch."

"Well, I may be able to find that out."

"How?"

"My lady knows them hoes. I just found out, and I can probably get that information out of her for you."

"Handle it, my nigga. Get me that information, and I'ma bless you, my dude."

"Relax, my nigga. I fuck with you, so I'ma handle this as soon as I get at my lady."

"I owe you, my dude."

Hanging up the phone with Fish Man, with a smile on his face and shaking his head, Rob instantly forgot about the conversation he just had as soon as his phone rang again. He saw the name of the new female he just started fucking with now calling him.

13

Holding up the ringing cell phone and seeing both name and number blocked, Alinna walked over to stand beside Nicole, who was still tied to the wooden chair, and said, "Remember what I said. Find out where Monica's at in Florida City."

Nodding her head in understanding, Nicole saw Alinna hit the speaker button on the phone and answered the call: "Hello."

"Nicole, it's Monica. What took you so long to answer the phone?"

"Hey, Monica. I was inside the kitchen when you called. Erick just bought me the phone."

"How my brother-in-law doing?"

"He's alright," Nicole replied. She then paused a moment before she continued. "When are you coming back home?"

"Nicole, I already explained this to you. I'm not coming back until I finish what I'm doing."

"What exactly are you doing, Nicole?"

"Don't worry about it, Nicole. Just know that I'm safe, and when I'm done, I'll be home."

"Well, tell me where you are, so I can come and at least visit."

Quiet for a moment, Monica finally said, "That's not a good idea right now, Nicole."

"Why not? What the hell is going on, Monica? I don't under . . . ," Nicole burst out in tears, unable to finish what she was saying.

Tired of waiting, Alinna took the phone away from Nicole, placed it to her ear, and said, "How's it going, Monica? It's been a while since we last talked."

Quiet for a moment, Monica said, "What the hell you doing with my sister, you bitch? I swear if you do anything to—"

"I tell you what I want," Alinna began, cutting off Monica. "You get Dante out of jail and this case thrown out, and I'll release your sister and brother-in-law. You don't . . . and the next time you'll see her, she'll be a story on the news about a dead body being found. You got six seconds to think about it."

Alinna hung up the phone, just as James called out when he walked into the room. She looked over her shoulder as he walked in holding her cell phone. She then gave him a look.

"Dante!" James told her.

Taking the phone just as Nicole's phone started ringing again, Alinna told Dante to hold on. She then said, "It's either yes or no. Decide one now."

"Okay! Give me some time to try and work this out," Monica said, giving in to Alinna's demands.

"You've got twenty-four hours," Alinna answered, hanging up the phone and then holding up her phone back to her ear. "Hey, baby, what took you so long to call me?"

"I had to deal with a little problem in here that came up," Dante answered, but then asked, "Who was you just talking to just now?"

"The person that's getting you released from that place."

"Monica?"

"Yep."

"How'd you find . . . ?"

"I found her sister," Alinna told him. "I gave her twenty-four hours to get you released."

"That may just be a problem, Alinna."

"Why?"

"This state attorney has got his dick hard to fuck me, shorty! He's gonna fight against me being released."

"But with no witnesses to talk, what do they have, Dante?"

"I hear you, but the best way is to handle this state attorney to be sure."

"Hold on, Dante," Alinna told him, turning to face James. "James, go get Dre. Tell him I've got one more job for him and Wesley to handle."

* * *

"Hello," Senior DEA Agent Victor Murphy answered, half asleep.

Monica wasted no time saying, "Victor wake up. It's Monica. I need you to get the hell up now!"

"Whoa . . . ! What's the problem, Martin?" Murphy inquired, sounding more alert now.

"I need you to release Dante from jail. Drop the charges against him."

"What?" Agent Murphy yelled in both surprise and disbelief. "What are you talking about, Martin?"

"Victor, I'm on my way back to Miami now. Just trust me on this. I need you to get Dante Blackwell released from jail and his charges dropped. I can't really explain right now, but I really need you to do this for me."

"Shit!" Agent Murphy shouted, sighing loudly over the phone. Sounding as if he was moving around, he finally said, "Alright, but it's going to take me some time to get this done . . . if I can get it done. But as soon as you get here, I want to know exactly what the hell is going on."

"I will," Monica promised. "Also, Victor, we've only got twenty-four hours to have Dante released . . . and the clock is already ticking."

* * *

Alinna was at home and lying in bed with D.J. when Dre called to let her know that the state attorney was no longer an issue. He told her that he and his family decided to go on a faraway boat trip, diving in deep waters. Alinna hung up with Dre with a smile on her face. Her phone rang again and she answered, "Yeah."

"Alinna, this Vanessa. We've got a problem."

"What now, Vanessa?"

"It's Harmony. She's in the hospital. I don't know what happened, but Keisha just called me a few minutes ago saying something about Harmony needing to go to the hospital with some bad bleeding or something."

"What hospital she at, Vanessa?" Alinna asked as she climbed out of bed.

Alinna hung up the phone with Vanessa after she found out the hospital at which Harmony was admitted. She quickly got dressed and woke up Ms. Rose to take care of D.J. She then woke up James, who was on the other side of the house.

The two of them left the house five minutes later, with James driving Dante's Mercedes-Benz. Alinna pulled out her phone and called Tony T, making sure he was told what was going on with Harmony.

"What's up? Who this?"

"Tony T . . . this Alinna. Where you at?"

"I was just handling some business just now. Why? What's up?"

"You need to get to Jackson Memorial Hospital. Harmony in the hospital, boy."

"What the fuck you . . . !"

Hearing the click of the phone in the middle of what Tony T was saying, Alinna looked at her phone to see that

Tony T had hung up. She shook her head as she put down her phone.

* * *

Alinna and James arrived at Jackson Memorial Hospital about fifteen minutes after she hung up with Tony T. They entered the hospital parking lot, ran through the front entrance, and rushed over to the elevators.

Taking the elevator to the fourth floor, both Alinna and James stepped off and rushed up the hallway to room 107. Finding the others all crowded in front of the room, Alinna had barely stopped, when Tony T came flying around the corner.

"What the fuck happen to my girl?" Tony T yelled, face balled up in anger.

"Relax, Tony T!" Vanessa told him calmly, showing a small smile. "Harmony's okay."

"What do you mean, she alright?" Tony T asked, looking from Vanessa to Alinna and then to the others, only to find himself looking back at Vanessa.

"The doctor's in there with her now, and we don't know what was wrong with her. But we do know that she's not in any danger. The doctor told us that much," Vanessa broke down, explaining for Tony T just as Harmony's room door opened and the doctor stepped out. She stopped the middle-aged man and asked, "So what's the word, Doctor?"

"Well, as I told you all before," the doctor began, looking around at all the faces outside his patient's room, "Ms. Harrison will be just fine. But she needs to take it easy as her pregnancy continues further along."

"Whoa . . . !" Tony T said as he walked up to the doctor, stopping only a few inches from him. "What the hell you just say? Pregnancy?"

"Yes, sir," the doctor replied. "Ms. Harrison is two and a half months pregnant."

Vanessa moved toward Tony T, realizing he was just moments from losing it. Alinna then led him into Harmony's room and then thanked the doctor as he walked away.

*   *   *

Stepping back in the hallway outside of Harmony's hospital room, Keisha checked her cell phone to see if she had any missed phone calls or voice messages from Rob.

Trying Rob's number again, Keisha stood a moment listening to the number ringing until his voicemail picked up. She hung up and was about to shut off her phone, when it rang inside her hand. Smiling at seeing Rob's phone number on her screen, she answered, "Hey, baby!"

"Ummm . . . ! Who is this?"

Caught off guard by the woman's voice, and looking at her cell screen again to see Rob's name and number, Keisha got back on the phone and said, "Who the fuck is this? Where is Rob?"

"Rob's in the shower right now . . . and this is his woman you're talking to. Who the hell are you?"

"His woman, huh?" Keisha asked, laughing lightly. "Well, do me a favor. Tell Rob I said to lose my number."

Hanging up the phone, Keisha stood where she was a few moments. She was thinking about what the hell had just happened, when she heard behind her, "You alright?"

Turning around, she saw Alinna walking out of the hospital room. Keisha nodded her head and was just about to lie and say that she was doing alright. But she then remembered that she wanted to asked Alinna something about Rob. "Alinna, do you know somebody named Rob?"

"Which Rob you talking about?" Alinna asked, staring a little harder at Keisha.

"His real name is Robert Bell."

"You mean the same Rob that sells weed and coke?"

"He just sell coke now," Keisha corrected Alinna and then added, "Earlier today, he asked me about you, and once before, Vanessa and Amber seen him at Vanessa's spot out in Fort Lauderdale."

"What the hell he doing over there?" Alinna asked, raising her voice a little and staring hard at Keisha.

Keisha explained how she had been seeing Rob for a few months and how she introduced him to Kyree on a business-type level. Keisha added, "I'm cutting his ass off, though. I just called his phone, and some bitch answered talking about she being his woman."

"Don't cut 'im off yet!" Alinna told Keisha with a smile. "Rob owes me from a fucked up business deal some time back. I want you to just hold on to him a little while, and I'll let you know what I need you to do for me."

"Well, I know he has a team he works with. Some guys from out of town. Some fat ugly nigga that goes by the name Fish Man."

"Wait, Keish!" Alinna cut in. "You say what the other nigga's name is?"

"Fish Man," Keisha repeated, now seeing a change of expression on Alinna's face.

"So his fat ass back in town after all, huh?" Alinna said more to herself. She then looked back toward Keisha and said, "Yeah, Keisha. Hold onto Rob just a little longer. I've got a plan."

*　*　*

Monica had received Agent Murphy's emergency message, but finally got the chance to call him back after checking into a motel across town off of 27th Avenue and 79th Street. She stood in front of her motel window listening to the line ring a moment before he answered, "Martin, this you?"

"Yeah, Victor. What you got?"

"I don't know what the hell is going on, but the state attorney also has gone missing now. What in God's name is going on?"

Alinna Rodriguez doing what she needs to, to get Dante out of jail, Monica thought, but responded to Agent Murphy, "Whatever's going on, Victor, we'll get to the bottom of it. Did you get the judge to release Dante from jail yet?"

"I spoke with a few people who spoke with Judge Thomas. They explained that the DEA was dropping the charges against Dante Blackwell, and the response I got back was that once the judge spoke with the state, we would get an answer."

"But you just said that the state attorney is missing."

"And that's why the judge signed the release on Blackwell," Agent Murphy told Monica. "Blackwell should be out of jail within two or three hours."

"I'll call you back, Victor," Monica said, hanging up the phone just as Agent Murphy yelled her name.

Monica quickly called her sister's phone number. After two rings, she heard Alinna's voice over the phone: "I better hear something good."

"Dante's being released in a few hours," Monica told her, but then asked, "Now will you release my sister?"

"Call me back once Dante is released, and then I'll tell you where you can meet your family."

Upon hearing Alinna hang up the phone, Monica caught herself before slinging her cell phone across the room. Instead, she took a deep breath and slowly released it.

She then called Agent Murphy back. He answered on the start of the second ring as Monica said, "Victor . . . it's Monica."

"Martin! What the hell is going on here?" Murphy demanded, yelling into the phone.

Sighing deeply, Monica told Agent Murphy about her family being kidnapped by Dante Blackwell's fiancée and about Alinna Rodriguez's demands of Dante's release and all charges being dropped against him.

"So let's just arrest his fiancée after we get your family back. We can even get the FBI in on this case, and then go after Blackwell again."

"Victor, if you lay one hand on Alinna Rodriquez, Dante will lose it. He's a thinker and a planner, but he's a first-rate murderous fool. But I've learned that if there's one thing he will completely lose it over, it's Alinna Rodriguez. It will be a murderous day or week, until he is no longer breathing, but then Alinna is just as bad as he is. So we may be just talking about starting the largest murderous season Miami has ever seen. Believe me when I say that both Dante Blackwell and Alinna Rodriguez aren't alone and have a lot of help behind them."

"So what the hell are we supposed to do? We can't just let these bastards get away with what they're doing!"

"We're not, Victor," Monica said to Agent Murphy while already planning inside her head. "But for now, we just let them think we're backing off. Let things cool off. But we'll keep a watch on them, and then build a bigger and stronger case than before."

"You sound as if you're coming back to the agency, Martin."

"You offering me back my job, Victor?"

"I've still got your gun and shield in my desk drawer. It's here when you get here."

"I'll be in in a few hours," Monica told him, but then asked, "What about Angela? You still have a tail on her?"

Quiet a moment, Agent Murphy replied, "I figured since you were ending the case on Blackwell . . ."

"You pulled the tail on Angela, didn't you, Victor?"

"You want me to put them back on her?"

"I'll let you know. I'll call you later, Victor," Monica told Agent Murphy, hanging up the phone.

14

Alinna and James sat out front of the Miami-Dade County Jail inside the metallic black and chrome-edged new model Bentley Continental GT Speed that Alinna had bought for Dante. Behind the dark-tinted windows, she ignored the crowd that was growing around the car, with cameras taking pictures and cameramen and news reporters yelling over each other, trying to be heard.

"Alinna! There we go now!" James said, nodding to the front doors of the jail.

Alinna broke out in a huge smile seeing Dante with his team of lawyers. He was dressed in a pearl-white Kenneth Cole suit with a sky-blue button-up Kenneth Cole shirt. She controlled herself until James finally opened her door for her. She climbed out just as Dante approached the Bentley.

"What's up, shorty?" Dante said, smirking as he stopped in front of her. "You miss your man or what?"

Laughing as she wrapped her arms up and around his neck, Alinna laid in against Dante hugging him. Sighing after his arms wrapped around her waist, she said, "I missed you so much, boy! Let's get out of here."

Allowing Alinna to lead him into the Bentley by the hand, Dante touched fists with a smiling James and said, "What's up, playboy?"

"What's up, bruh. Good to have you back," James said as he was closing the car door behind Dante and Alinna.

"You look good!" Dante told Alinna, leaning over and kissing her on the lips.

Alinna pulled out of the kiss after only a few moments. Feeling the dam between her legs open up and her wetness pouring out of her womanhood, she breathlessly said, "Wait, Dante. Let's not start right now, because if we start, believe me when I tell you that I won't be able to stop what I want to do to you."

Laughing lightly, Dante said, "Alright, shorty! Tell me what's going on. Where we at?"

First she told Dante about Monica and what was going on with her sister and brother-in-law, and that soon she'd be expecting a call from Monica that he had been released. Alinna then began to explain about losing track of Angela once everyone went to the hospital after Harmony had an emergency, finding out she was two months pregnant with Tony T's baby.

"Harmony alright?" Dante asked while staring out the car window.

"She's fine," Alinna answered, staring at Dante and expecting him to be upset about the loss of Angela. She was surprised when he looked over at her and his expression was calm.

"Anything else?" Dante asked her before calling up front to James and asking, "Pull over so I can get something to smoke, playboy."

"James . . . hand me that tote bag," Alinna said as James reached over to the passenger seat, picked up the black leather tote bag, and handed it back to her. She, in turn, handed it over to Dante and said, "This is for you."

Alinna watched as Dante opened the tote bag and saw the two boxes of Black & Milds, one vanilla and the other regular; a black and chrome flick lighter; and two twin Glock 45s facing each other in the bottom of the bag. Alinna then spoke up: "I've got some more news for you."

"I'm listening," Dante said after lighting up one of the Blacks and then taking out the two Glocks and checking them.

"I've found Rob," she told Dante. "You remember Rob, right?"

"Ain't he the clown that used to cop from you some time back?"

"Yeah, that's him. But guess who else I found as well?" Alinna asked. Before Dante could even reply, she said, "Fish Man ass back in town too."

Cutting his eyes over at Alinna and meeting her eyes a moment, Dante shook his head and focused back on his two new bangers before saying, "Call Vanessa and tell her I said to bring that over to your old spot at the apartments."

Doing as she was asked, Alinna pulled out her cell phone and dialed Vanessa's number.

"Hello!"

"Vaness . . . this is Alinna. Dante wants you . . . ," she began, before pulling her ear away from a screaming Vanessa on the other end. Alinna smiled and shook her head. She then handed the phone over to Dante and said, "She wants to talk to you."

Smiling as he took the phone from Alinna, and still hearing Vanessa screaming on the other end, Dante hung up the phone. He then texted her and told her that he was calling back and for her to stop screaming so they could talk.

He then called her back a few minutes later. Vanessa answered on the first ring: "Dante, you on the phone?"

"Yeah, Vanessa. What's up, sis?"

"Oh my God, boy! I missed you so much!"

"I missed you too, Nessa. Listen though, I need you to meet me at you and Alinna's old spot at the apartment, but bring what I had you hold for me, alright?"

"Alright, big bruh. I'm happy you're back too."

"I'm happy I'm back, Nessa," Dante replied, hanging up the phone and smiling. He handed the phone back to Alinna and said, "What's up?"

"Nothing," Alinna answered, shaking her head but still smiling. "So what are you planning to do about Fish Man and Rob?"

"I'll let you deal with Rob, but I got something for Fish Man," Dante told Alinna. "Where Natalie at though?"

"She flew back to Phoenix to pick up Carmen," Alinna answered just as her cell phone started to ring. She looked down at the screen and saw that it was Dre calling. She then answered, "What's up, Dre?"

"I've got Monica on a three-way," Dre told Alinna as he then called out to Monica.

"I'm here," Monica answered. "You got what you wanted, Alinna. Now where can I pick up my sister and brother-in-law?"

"I'll let you know," Alinna started. "But there are a few things I want to do before I tell you where they are at, just in case you're planning some—"

"Hang up the phone, Alinna," Dante ordered, cutting off Alinna from what she was saying.

Alinna hung up the phone as soon as Dante told her. She looked back to Dante as he said, "You said what you said. Don't spend too much time talking to her on the phone. You could be recorded and don't know it."

"She's not with the DEA anymore, Dante," Alinna told him.

"You really sure about that?" Dante asked, staring into Alinna's eyes, wanting her to think for herself.

*   *   *

Making it to Alinna's old spot where she and the girls used to stash their work, Dante noticed Vanessa's Benz truck as James was parking the Bentley.

Climbing from the car and holding the door open for Alinna, Dante closed the car door behind her and then followed alongside Alinna, with James on her right. He noticed how James looked around the parking area, using only his eyes.

Once they were upstairs and walked up to the apartment door, Alinna unlocked and opened it just as Vanessa came rushing out, almost knocking Alinna over to get to Dante.

"God damn, Nessa!" Alinna said, staring hard at Vanessa as she pulled away from James, who caught her from falling over. "You just gonna knock me down, bitch?"

"You was in the way!" Vanessa replied, smiling as she was hanging from around Dante's neck.

"Whatever!" Alinna said, rolling her eyes just as she heard, "Daddy!"

Hearing his daughter's voice, he looked inside the apartment to see Mya rushing at him with a huge smile on her face. Dante quickly released Vanessa and squatted down just as Mya slammed into him, wrapping her arms around his neck.

"Daddy, when you get home?" Mya asked, smiling as she pulled back a little to look up at him.

"Today, baby girl!" Dante answered, picking up his daughter before he entered the apartment.

Alinna smiled at the sight of Dante with his daughter and then followed them inside. She then walked into the front room and saw a 38-inch flat screen television playing the movie *Ice Age*.

Dante sat with his daughter a few minutes on the brown sofa, and then he looked over at Vanessa once Mya focused on the movie, and asked, "Nessa, where he at?"

"He in the bedroom," Vanessa answered, nodding toward the back bedroom.

Dante looked back down at Mya as she lay against his side, watching TV and smiling. Dante bent down and kissed the top of his daughter's head and said, "Baby girl, I'ma be right back. Stay with Auntie Nessa, alright?"

Standing up from the sofa beside Mya, Dante started toward the back bedroom, with Alinna and James right behind him.

Dante saw two females who looked alike as soon as he entered the bedroom. But he then shifted his eyes over to the guy standing in front of the bedroom window looking out, who turned and faced him at the sound of the bedroom door opening. Dante slowly smirked at the guy and said, "We meet again, Geno. Where's Angela at?"

"Man, I do . . . I don't know!"

"Be careful!" Dante said, interrupting Geno as the guy was trying to talk. He pulled off his suit jacket and handed it over to Alinna behind him. As he began unbuttoning his shirt, he continued, "You've got only one choice . . . and that's to tell me what I want to know, and then deal with what's about to happen to you, since you like lying to me and touching my daughter."

Alinna smiled a bit as she took Dante's shirt. She noticed that he looked bigger and even better built as she took note of the muscles on his naked back. She looked over at both Keisha and Maxine, who were staring hard at Dante. Even though she noticed their stares at him, she just shook her head and smiled. She then quickly turned her attention back to Dante and Angela's husband, as she heard Geno scream out in pain. She then saw Geno flying backward, slamming into the bedroom window and causing it to break with a loud exploding sound, knocking him out.

*   *   *

121

"No disrespect, Alinna, but Dante is too fine," Keisha told her as she, Maxine, Alinna, and James sat in the front room with Vanessa and Dante's daughter. Dante was in the bathroom, cleaning up the blood he got on himself after beating up Angela's husband, Geno.

"He is sexy as hell, Alinna!" Maxine said, adding on to what her sister said, before cutting her eyes over toward James and catching the look he shot her.

"Believe me, ladies . . . I'm used to the attention that Dante receives from women," Alinna began. She was still smiling when she turned around and saw Dante entering the room, drying off his hands on a towel.

"I'm ready to eat now," Dante said as he stood beside Alinna at the end of the sofa. But quickly he turned to the twins and asked, "Who are you two?"

"Dante, those two are the twins I told you about that Vanessa brought to the family along with their brother, Kyree," Alinna informed Dante. She then introduced Keisha first and then Maxine, who was seated next to and leaning into James.

Looking from Keisha over to Maxine and then back to Keisha, Dante said, "So you two are the ones that got the information out of the two detectives, huh? I've heard some good stuff about the two of you. I'll remember that."

"So what now?" Alinna asked, staring up at Dante beside her. "Geno gave us two places where Angela could be. Which do we check first?"

Dante remained quiet for a few moments, staring at his daughter asleep on Vanessa's lap. He then stood up and after a few minutes said, "We about to take a trip to Puerto Rico."

"So that's where you think she went?" Alinna asked, seeing Dante slowly nodding his head.

"Why stay in the States when you can leave and go back home where you think nobody can find you at?" Dante said, staring at nothing, deep in thought.

"So we're waiting until Geno wakes up to find out exactly where in Puerto Rico she went?" Alinna asked Dante just as her cell phone went off.

Pulling out her phone, she saw that it was Natalie calling. She then looked up to see that Dante was gone. She shook her head and smiled as she answered the phone, "Yeah, Natalie."

"Alinna, I'm back in Miami. Where's Dante?"

"Working . . . but go ahead and head over to the house. We'll be there in a little while. Carmen with you, right?"

"She's with me, but she wants to talk to Dante."

"He's in the middle of something, but I'll have him call you as soon as he's finished."

After talking with Natalie a few more minutes, Alinna hung up the phone with her. She then looked over at Keisha and called out, "What's up, Keisha?"

"I just hung up with Rob, and he wants to see me tonight," Keisha told Alinna, smiling a devilish grin. "What you want me to do?"

Looking at Dante as he reentered the room, Alinna met his eyes and held them for a moment. She then looked back at Keisha and said, "Go out with him, but I've got a plan that I want you to follow through with."

* * *

Hanging up with Keisha after she called him back and agreed to hook up and go out that night, Rob quickly called Fish Man's phone.

"Who this is?" Fish Man sounded pissed off when answering the phone.

"My nigga, what's up?" Rob asked, hearing the tone of his boy's voice. "Everything good? We got problems or something?"

"Nigga, you ain't been paying attention or something?"

"Fuck is you talking about?"

"Fool . . . instead of chasing these hoes, you should be paying attention to what's going on in the streets and on the news."

"Again, nigga. What the fuck is you talking about?"

Sighing loudly into the phone, Fish Man said, "Dude, if you wasn't my nigga, I wouldn't waste my muthafucking time. This bitch ass nigga Dante found some muthafucking way to get those crackers to let him out of jail . . . and even got all his charges dropped. And guess who was right there to pick his punk ass up . . . ? Alinna's bitch ass!"

Unable to respond and surprised at what Fish Man just told him, Rob said, "Let me hit you back." He then quickly hung up the phone.

"I gotta get the fuck outta here," Rob said as he jumped from his bed and then went through his apartment to quickly pack a bag.

15

Dante realized that Alinna really went all the way out with the buying of the new house that was, in fact, a huge mansion. He then cut his eyes over at a smiling Alinna as she slid across the seat and leaned against him. He turned his attention back out the window, watching as James drove up the long drive after passing through the tall front security gates. He then noticed security walking the grounds of the mansion.

Dante stared at the amount of space and the size of the mansion as James made his way around to the back end of the property. Dante slowly smiled at seeing his family already crowded out in front of the five-car garage.

As soon as James parked the Bentley, Dante climbed out. Just as Vanessa was parking beside him, she saw Dre's Land Rover and Tony T's Aston Martin also parked on the side of the garage. Dante held open the car door as Alinna climbed out, and he heard his son's voice shout: "Daddy."

Dante stepped around Alinna just as his son came rushing around the back end of the Bentley. He scooped up D.J., which caused his son to burst into a fit of laughter, as he asked, "What's up, little man?"

"Hi, Daddy!" D.J. said, hugging Dante's neck tightly.

"D.J.!" Mya cried at the sight of her brother. She broke away from Vanessa and rushed toward both her brother and father.

Picking up Mya in his left arm while still holding D.J. in his right, Dante smiled and said, "What happened to you two? Ya'll done got big as hell while I was gone."

"Excuse me, Dante," Rose began, standing over with the others and staring at him with a disapproving look on her face. "You will not speak that type of language around these babies. Are we clear?"

Cutting his eyes over to Alinna, who looked away smiling, Dante looked back to the older woman and heard, "Did you not understand me, Mr. Dante Blackwell?"

"Ummm . . . yes ma'am, Ms. Rose," Dante answered as Rose left the group and walked over to him, first taking the kids and then going up on her toes and kissing him on the cheek. "It's good to have you back home, sweetie."

"Come on, Dante!" Alinna told him, smiling and taking his arm. She led him over to the others and continued, "That's the new Ms. Rose. She's now in charge of the whole house and the entire staff that take care of everything."

Dante embraced his boys and hugged the girls until he reached Natalie, who stood smiling up at him with tears running down her face. Dante gently pulled her into him, wrapping his arms around her while she wrapped her arms up around his neck and hugged him tight as she cried into his neck.

Dante saw Natalie wasn't about to release him anytime soon, so he held her in his left arm. He then turned his focus on her mother, seeing Carmen standing to his right, smiling while also allowing tears to run down her face.

"Hey, Carmen," Dante spoke first, only for her to rush at him, throwing herself into him. She hugged him as tightly as she could. In turn, he wrapped his right arm around the older woman, holding both her and her daughter, unaware of the way that Alinna was watching him.

* * *

Dante walked with Natalie and Carmen while Alinna showed him through the huge mansion. When they came upon the guest quarters, he accepted a kiss on his cheek from

Carmen, who said goodbye for then. Natalie remained at his side as they continued on the tour of the mansion.

Finally ending up the mansion tour in the master bedroom, Dante caught the cut of Alinna's eyes as she shot Natalie a look, as she continued holding onto him. He saw a few more stares from Alinna at both Natalie and at him as well.

Dante released Natalie and slowly walked through the nice-sized bedroom. He then checked out the master bathroom with the his-and-hers baths, morning kitchen, dramatic shower overlooking the private gardens, and the designer closets that were already packed with his and Alinna's clothing. Dante looked behind him and heard Alinna ask, "So what do you think?"

Dante turned around and walked back over to Alinna as she stood staring at him. He bent down, kissed her, and said, "You did your thing, shorty! I like it up in here and the whole setup. You got it put together in here."

"I'm glad you—"

"Dante . . . ," Natalie called out, interrupting Alinna as she was talking, to get Dante's attention. "I've bought you something. Let's go out back so I can show you."

Catching the look that Alinna shot him as he allowed Natalie to pull him out of the bathroom, Dante knew he was going to have to talk with both Natalie and Alinna . . . and very soon.

Once outside and passing through the back part of the mansion, Dante saw D.J., Mya, and A.J. playing inside the fenced backyard. Dante followed Natalie through the fence gate as she led him through a walkway and onto a floating dock with an additional lift and watercraft floating pad. He stopped a moment later beside Natalie and looked up at a huge boat.

"So what do you think, baby?" Natalie asked, smiling as she waved her hand out over the boat. "It's your gift I bought you. It's a sixty-foot luxury yacht. Do you like it?"

"Hell yeah, woman!" Dante answered as he scooped up Natalie in his arms, causing her to scream playfully and go into a fit of giggling while he carried her onto the yacht.

*   *   *

Alinna watched Dante as he carried a giggling Natalie onto the new yacht she had bought him. She noticed the way that he reacted to Natalie and the way the two of them reacted to each other. Alinna felt tears slowly begin to slide down her face at the realization of how much Dante was really in love with someone other than just her.

"You alright, Alinna?"

Brushing away the tears at hearing someone behind her, Alinna turned around only to find herself face-to-face with Carmen.

"I'm fine, Carmen," Alinna told the woman, forcing a smile. "Is everything okay with you? Do you need anything?"

"Sweetheart, can I say something to you that I'm sure you need to hear?" Carmen asked, ignoring Alinna's question about her well-being.

"Go ahead, Carmen," Alinna told the older woman, seeing the seriousness in her face.

"Dante loves you, Alinna," Carmen started, pausing a moment while holding the younger woman's eyes. "Dante and I have had long talks, and he has told me a great deal about you and even how the two of you first met. But it was when Dante made the decision to deal with Angela that the two of you began to have trouble in your relationship. As a man, Dante knows his mistake was not agreeing to this

Angela woman's terms, but when he kept the truth from you is when he made his mistake. As a woman, I can understand your feelings and your reactions to finding out about Angela and Dante. But tell me something, Alinna. Why do you think Dante made the decisions he made and is still making?"

"To protect me."

"Why is that?"

"Because . . . because he loves me," Alinna answered, crying freely now.

Pulling Alinna into her arms and holding the younger woman, Carmen spoke again after a moment: "Alinna, Dante loves you. Trust me when I tell you this. But when you kicked him out of your life, you allowed someone else to accept him into theirs. Natalie loves Dante just as much as you do, but now it's time for you to make a decision, Alinna. Do you love Dante enough to accept him as he is and what faults he has, or are you willing to give him up completely?"

"I love Dante too much. I'm not letting him go again," Alinna replied, talking more to herself than to Carmen.

*　　*　　*

Standing in the shower, letting the hot water beat down on his back, neck, and shoulders, Dante stood thinking about different things that were crowding his mind. He gave up after a little while, trying to get his thoughts in order.

Shutting off the shower, Dante opened the shower door, grabbed his towel from behind the door, dried off, and stepped out of the shower.

He put on his silk panda boxers and then put on his Hanes wife beater. Dante left the bathroom, walked back out into the bedroom, and headed over to his dresser, when he heard the bedroom door open.

He lifted his eyes and looked into the mirror above his dresser to see Alinna entering the bedroom. She was staring at him, dressed in his T-shirt. Dante focused back on what he was doing: spraying on some Polo body spray that Alinna had bought for him.

"Dante, we need to talk," Alinna told him as she climbed into the oversized bed.

Lifting his eyes again to look back at Alinna through the mirror, and meeting her eyes, Dante sighed as he set down the spray bottle. He turned around and walked over to the bed, sat down beside Alinna, and said, "Alright. I already know what this is about, Alinna. What do you want me to do? We agreed she—"

"Will you let me speak first, please?" Alinna asked, cutting off Dante in the middle of what he was trying to say. She rolled her eyes as she continued, "Like I was about to say. I'm not stupid, Dante. I can see that Natalie is really in love with you, and you're in love with—"

"Alinna, it's . . ."

"Shut up, Dante," Alinna said, raising her voice as she gave him a look. "I can see that you're in love with her also, Dante. I saw that clearly today while you two were together out on that new yacht she bought you. But I've said all of that to say this. I still stand by what we agreed on about Natalie coming to live with us. But there's something that's happening too."

"What's that?"

"You're going to marry the both of us," Natalie said, causing Dante to swing his head around and stare straight at her standing inside the bedroom, in front of the closed bedroom door.

"What the hell?" Dante asked, looking from Natalie and swinging his head back around to Alinna. "What's going on, Alinna?"

"What's going on is exactly what Natalie just told you now," Alinna replied, looking at Natalie as she was now climbing into the bed beside her. She looked at Dante again and said, "I want you to marry me . . . and Natalie wants the same thing."

"How do you two expect to . . . ?" Dante paused in mid-sentence, staring at Alinna to Natalie and back again to Alinna. Both women were smiling at him as he continued, "I'm supposed to marry Alinna here in the US and then go to the Dominican Republic and marry Natalie?"

"He catches on quick, doesn't he?" Alinna said, smiling over at Natalie.

"Let's see if he can quickly catch on to what we want now, Alinna," Natalie said, smiling as both she and Alinna crawled under the covers together and stared at Dante.

Dante watched both women as the T-shirt that Alinna was wearing was pulled off. Then Natalie tossed her silk button-up night shirt and her matching shorts onto the floor. Dante sat up and stared for a moment before he was climbing onto the bed and moving in between both of the women.

*   *   *

Dante switched back and forth, first kissing Alinna and then Natalie as they both ran their hands over him, pulling off his wife beater and boxers. They worked as a team against him, and Dante found himself forced onto his back. He then looked up at Natalie as she climbed on top of him and soon straddled his head. He met her eyes a moment before she lowered her dripping pussy down onto his face.

Dante began licking Natalie the way she always really enjoyed. He gripped her by the waist and held her in place as he locked his lips onto her clit, sucking just hard enough to cause her to grab hold of his head with both hands, crying out his name. He then slid his tongue between the lips of her womanhood, feeling her womanly liquid flooding into his mouth.

"Oh shit!" Dante cried out, almost choking on Natalie's liquid as he felt Alinna's lips tightly wrap around his manhood, sucking him deep.

"Dante . . . please!" Natalie cried, gripping his head and grinding her pussy on his lips.

Dante was working on Natalie while Alinna was working on him. He was trying hard to focus on what he was doing to Natalie until she cried out his name. He could feel her climax as he tried to catch as much of her liquid that was now pouring out of her, before she fell over to his side and onto the bed, breathing hard and smiling with her eyes closed.

"Ready for me, handsome?" Alinna asked as she climbed onto Dante, straddling his lower half, staring into his eyes as she led him inside of her. "Oh God . . . Yesss, Dante!"

Riding Dante hard, Alinna could feel him deep inside of her stomach as she gripped his muscular chest. Alinna then held his eyes as she continued riding him. She shifted her eyes over to Natalie as the other woman crawled over and began kissing Dante on the lips.

Alinna watched Dante and Natalie kiss. As Dante reached out for her breasts, Alinna cried out as she rode him harder, actually getting more excited watching the two of them.

Breaking the kiss with Dante to look up at Alinna after hearing her cry out, Natalie lay watching her a few moments. She then reached out and took Alinna's right hand into hers. Feeling Alinna grip her hand tight, both women locked eyes a moment, until Alinna's eyes rolled back into her head and she cried out, "Oh God . . . Danteeeee!"

*   *   *

As Dante lay in bed between both Alinna and Natalie, both ladies asleep on each side of his chest, Dante lay awake just thinking about everything that was going on at the moment. His thoughts turned from Angela and her bullshit to Monica and even Fish Man, who was an ongoing problem that he was supposed to have already handled a long time ago.

Dante slowly crawled out from under Alinna and then Natalie. He climbed out of bed and made his way into the bathroom and into the shower.

Dante turned on both the hot and cold faucets, stood under the water, and leaned against the shower wall, when he heard the bathroom door open. A moment later, the shower door opened behind him.

"You okay?" Alinna asked as she wrapped her arms around him from behind. "Something on your mind, isn't it?"

"Yeah," Dante answered as he slowly turned around and faced her, still inside her arms. He wrapped his arms loosely around her. "I'm just putting together everything inside of my head. I'm planning out a few different other ideas, trying to decide which ones I am going to go with."

"Well, I should tell you now then," Alinna said, lifting her head to look up at Dante. "Keisha got a call from Rob earlier today. She supposed to meet up with him, and she was supposed to call me and let me know where they at later on tonight."

"What you planning?"

"First, I'ma find out exactly where Fish Man is, but then after that, I'ma make good on my promise to kill his ass!"

Nodding his head in response, Dante stood quietly thinking a moment but then focused back on Alinna, saying,

"We'll handle this marriage in the morning down at the justice building, but then we need to see about renting a jet or something . . ."

"Whoa!" Alinna said, stopping Dante in the middle of what he was saying. "We don't need to rent no jet. Natalie has one, and she wants to go with us when we leave for Puerto Rico."

"Naw . . . ," Dante said, shaking his head. "Natalie isn't coming to Puerto—"

"Dante! First . . . it's her jet and, secondly, you just got back home . . . and she was the one taking care of things out here with me while you was away," Alinna broke in, explaining to Dante and cutting him off. "If she wants to go, I really don't see how you are going to stop her!"

"Where's Gomez?" Dante asked, angrily shaking his head, unable to believe the bullshit he was hearing.

Smiling at seeing Dante give in, but pretty sure he was going to all but threaten Gomez about Natalie's safety while they were away in Puerto Rico, Alinna asked, "Dante, what about Monica and Fish Man? We're just going to leave while there are still problems here?"

"I've been thinking about that," Dante admitted. "Right now there's a lot of attention on not just me, but on all of us. People are missing, and I just walked right out of jail scot-free after facing a death or life sentence for murdering two law enforcement officers. People are going to be expecting shit to start jumping off now that I'm back home. So we're going to do the opposite. Let everybody think we're not going to react to the bullshit. And with Angela out of the country, that'll give us time to disappear for a while."

Nodding her head in agreement and understanding exactly what Dante was explaining, Alinna asked, "So we're getting married tomorrow, huh?"

Smiling as he shook his head at Alinna, Dante bent his head down and kissed her. Afterward, he said, "Yeah, Mrs. Blackwell. Tomorrow you will be Alinna Blackwell."

16

Natalie woke up to find Dante and Alinna gone, leaving her alone inside their bed. She climbed out of bed and went back to her own bedroom on the other side of the mansion, where she took a shower and then got dressed.

When she was done, she left the bedroom and made her way to the kitchen, where she found Rose cooking while Harmony and Vanessa were eating at the breakfast bar with D.J., Mya, and A.J.

"Hey, Natalie girl. We thought you was going to sleep the whole morning!" Harmony said, smiling over at the woman who was having another one of Dante's baby.

"Are you eating, Natalie?" Rose asked as she was stepping around another one of the chefs who was preparing food.

"Thank you, Rose," Natalie told her before turning back to Vanessa and Harmony and asking, "Do either of you know where Dante or Alinna went to?"

"They left earlier this morning," Vanessa told her. "Dante just said that they would be back later."

"They didn't say where they were going?" Natalie asked, looking from Vanessa to Harmony and then back to Vanessa.

"Sorry, Natalie . . . Dante just said that they would be back later," Vanessa repeated just as Rose was setting down a plate of food in front of Natalie as both Dre and Wesley entered the kitchen.

A little upset that Dante and Alinna would leave without at least telling her what they were about to do, Natalie tried to ignore the feeling as she sat down to eat her breakfast. Just then, her mother walked into the kitchen holding her cell phone up to her ear.

When Natalie saw the expression on her mother's face, she shook her head sadly, knowing Carmen was on the phone with her father.

"What's up everybody?" Tony T said as he entered the kitchen all hyped up. He stopped next to Harmony, kissed her on the cheek, and then asked, "Where my nigga Dante at?"

"He and Alinna left this morning to handle something," Harmony told her man as she continued to eat her food.

"Well, when he say he coming back?" Tony T asked. "We got some business to discuss."

"What business?" Harmony and Natalie both asked, giving Tony T a look.

"Whoa . . . relax ya'll," Tony T told both ladies, holding up his hand in surrender. "It's legit business this time."

"What are you talking about, Tony T?" Vanessa asked as she sat down next to the women with a plate filled with food.

Looking back as Amber entered the kitchen, kissing Wesley on her way to the refrigerator, Tony T saw that everybody but Dante and Alinna were present, so he said, "It's like this, ya'll. I helped out this white dude a few months back when he was about to get robbed by a few dudes. I just happened to peep, and because I had a few of Harmony's young guns rolling with me, ain't shit go down with the white dude. Come to find out, though, homeboy was going through a little business deal problem on this club he was trying to pen out on South Beach. He couldn't get a partner to help out with the business, and then he was having some security problems . . ."

"Let me guess!" Vanessa spoke up, cutting off Tony T as he was explaining. "The homeboy you talking about is willing to pay you for security, right?"

"Let a nigga finish . . . damn!" Tony T said, shaking his head. "As a nigga was saying, I spoke with the white dude, and then I spoke with my nigga, Dante, who homeboy already heard of. Dante told me to make the guy an offer, and homeboy jumped all over it."

"What was the offer, Tony T?" Natalie asked him.

"Since we'll be handling security, Dante offered the white guy a sixty-forty split in ownership," Tony T told the others. "But he also put each of our names down as co-owners, so me, Dre, and Dante will split the forty percent among us."

"What about the girls?" Amber asked.

"What about the girls?" Dante asked as he followed Alinna inside the back door, with James following behind.

"Dante!" Natalie cried happily, jumping from her seat and rushing over to him.

Dante caught Natalie as she threw her arms around his neck. He accepted the kiss she gave him, but then asked with a smile, "So I guess you missed me this morning?"

"Where'd you go?" Natalie asked, pouting while still holding onto Dante.

"I'm let Alinna tell everybody, but Natalie come with me real quick," Dante told her, taking her hand. He then caught Alinna's eye, winking at her before leading Natalie outside.

"Alinna, what's going on?" Vanessa asked her best friend.

Smiling as she went inside her Burberry bag, Alinna pulled out a folded piece of paper. She then handed it over to Vanessa and said, "Read this."

Vanessa took the paper from Alinna, only for Harmony and Amber to slide in next to her to look over her shoulder. Vanessa then read. the paper, but she then froze once she began reading it.

"Oh shit, Alinna!" Harmony cried as she and Amber rushed over to hug her.

"What the hell is going on?" Dre asked, taking the paper from a now-crying Vanessa.

Leaving her seat to hug her girl, Vanessa wrapped her arms around Alinna and said, "Girl, I am so happy you finally married my brother crazy ass. It's about time!"

"It damn sure . . . ," came screams from outside as she was talking. Alinna took off first, with the rest of the family right behind her, busting out the door all behind each other.

"Everything good, fam?" Dante said, laughing as Natalie hugged him tight. He held her up as she held onto him, both her arms and legs wrapped around him.

"Natalie . . . what are you doing?" Carmen demanded as the others began putting away their guns and the security began disappearing.

"Mother . . . Dante gave me . . . Dante asked me . . ."

"I asked Natalie to marry me, Carmen," Dante finished her sentence. Natalie was too excited to talk and was now showing off the diamond ring he just bought for her after he and Alinna left the justice building. "I'm taking Natalie back to the Dominican Republic to get married."

"Oh, Dante! This is great new!" Carmen cried happily as she rushed over to Dante and hugged her soon-to-be son-in-law's neck.

"Since we're sharing the good news," Tony T spoke up loud enough to draw everyone's attention, he told Dante and Alinna about the new nightclub of which he, Dre, and Dante were now part owners. He then explained that tonight was the club's opening, and that they all should go out and celebrate.

"That's a good idea!" Natalie agreed, but then looked to Dante and asked, "Dante, can we go, baby? Please!"

Dante looked over at Alinna, who gave a slight nod of approval. Although he realized their flight to Puerto Rico would be pushed back another day, he said, "Yeah, Natalie. We can go out tonight."

Hearing her cell phone from inside her bag, Alinna dug out her iPhone and saw that Keisha was calling. "Yeah, Keisha. What's up?"

"Alinna, something's wrong. Rob never called me back last night or came to pick me up," Keisha told Alinna before explaining, "I went by his apartment and his car was gone, but his apartment still looks like it always does."

"Did you call or check on him this morning?"

"I'm just now leaving his apartment, and it's the same way as before."

"Alright, Keisha. I'ma handle it. Just call me later if you hear anything."

"What's up, shorty?" Dante asked, causing Alinna to jump in surprise as she was hanging up the phone.

Alinna was unaware that Dante had walked up to her. She'd have to get used to him appearing and disappearing again. As she turned to Dante, she said, "Keisha just called and said that Rob never called or showed up like he was supposed to. She went by his apartment and he wasn't there, but I'm guessing he's gone."

Nodding his head slowly, Dante said, "He found out I was home, but I'm pretty sure that's only part of the reason for his disappearing act. There's something going on, and I'ma figure it out."

"What are you planning, Dante?" Alinna asked, seeing the old look back on his face.

"Call Greg Wilson for me," Dante told Alinna just as Natalie walked over smiling up at him.

"Hey, you! What's wrong?" Natalie asked, noticing Dante's facial expression.

"Nothing!" Dante answered. "What's up? What's on your mind, beautiful?"

"Mother wants to talk to you," Natalie told him, taking his hand and leading him over to where her mother was standing and talking on the cell phone.

Dante saw the expression on Carmen's face before she focused on him. Her expression changed as she tried to give him a smile, so Dante winked his eye at her. Carmen reached out and gently laid her hand against the side of Dante's face as a huge genuine smile appeared on her face this time.

"Dante," Carmen said as she finally hung up the phone and had a big smile on her face, "I have a favor I want to ask of you."

"Anything, Carmen. What is it?"

"I want you to speak with Dominic," she told him, watching his face for his feeling toward her husband, only to find nothing but the same calm, extremely handsome face she always saw when she looked at Dante.

"You told him about me marrying Natalie?" Dante asked, holding Carmen's eyes.

Nodding her head slowly, Carmen said, "He's upset, Dante. He doesn't understand what's going on between you and Natalie, and then there's the fact that you just walked out of jail with all charges dropped, and he's also noticed that he has been watched."

"Watched?" Dante asked.

"He's not sure yet, but it's either the same people who were after you and your family, or it could be the FBI."

Nodding his head, Dante turned and looked over to where Alinna was standing with the rest of the family. He then called out her name to get her attention. He nodded for her to come over to where he and Natalie were standing with Carmen.

"Yeah, Dante," Alinna said as she walked up beside him. "What's wrong?"

"You still got contact with Monica?"

"Yeah, why?"

"Call her for me," Dante told Alinna. At the same time, he turned back toward Carmen and said, "Call Dominic back and tell him I'ma see what's going on, and then I'ma gonna take care of the problem. But make sure he understands that I'm doing this for you and Natalie. He and I will talk, though, and real soon."

"I'll let him know, Dante . . . and thank you," Carmen told him smiling.

"Dante!" Alinna called out as she handed him Monica's sister's phone. "It's Monica."

Taking the phone from Alinna, Dante stepped away from the ladies as he spoke into the phone: "Monica."

"What do you want, Dante?" Monica asked with much attitude when she heard his voice.

"I'm only saying this once, so listen clearly," Dante began in a calm and clear tone. "Whatever investigation you've got going on Dominic Saldana . . . end it now! If it's not you, then you find out who it is and get it ended!"

"I don't know what you're talking about."

"Find out . . . and call this number back in five minutes. I don't hear back from you, then I'll get involved with what Alinna has going on with your sister. You've got five minutes."

Hanging up the phone on Monica, Dante looked down at the new white and yellow diamond bezel Mickey Mouse Cartier watch that Alinna had bought for him a few hours ago, while they were buying Natalie's ring. It was 12:10 p.m.

Walking back over to Alinna, Dante handed her back the cell phone and said, "Monica's going to call in five minutes. Let me know what's she says."

* * *

Seeing her brother standing outside and in front of the trap spot he was running with four of his workers, Keisha parked her Infiniti Q50 behind Kyree's Chevy Impala, on which he had had work done.

"What's up, baby sis?" Kyree called out as Keisha climbed from the Infiniti.

"What's up, Kyree?" she replied as she walked inside the yard. "I need to talk to you."

"What about?" he asked, walking off with his sister, away from his workers. "Everything good with you, right?"

"I'm alright, Kyree, but I'm looking for Rob. You seen-"

"You just missed that nigga a few minutes before you pulled up," Kyree told her, cutting her off. "Everything good with you and that nigga?"

"Kyree, tell me you know where he was going," Keisha said, ignoring her brother's question.

"He ain't say," Kyree told her, staring hard at his sister. "What's going on, Keisha?"

"Alinna wants him," Keisha told her brother. She then explained the beef between Rob and Alinna . . . and even Fish Man.

"Well, I don't know where this bitch ass nigga Rob went at. He came by and re-upped. But I do know where this clown Fish Man open up one of his trap spots at," Kyree explained to his sister.

"Kyree, are you serious?" Keisha asked, smiling at her brother. She quickly pulled out her cell phone and called Alinna.

"Yeah, Keisha."

"Alinna, I got some good news. Kyree say he know where Fish Man got one of his trap houses at. You wanna talk to him?"

"Put him on the phone, Keisha."

143

"Alinna wanna talk to you," Keisha told her brother as she handed him the phone.

Taking the phone from his sister, Kyree spoke into the cell, "What's up, Alinna?"

"Kyree . . . hold on. I'm putting Dante on the phone," Alinna told him. Dante came over the line a moment later: "Yeah!"

Kyree remained quiet for a moment, in shock at the thought of actually being on the phone with Dante Blackwell, the same nigga who got niggas in the streets. He pulled himself together after hearing Dante say his name and said, "Yeah, Dante. I'm here, boss man."

"What you gotta tell me, young'n?"

"My sister say you looking for that nigga Fish Man. I know where one of his spots at."

"So you the twins' brother, right?"

"Yes, sir."

"Kyree, right?"

"Yes, sir."

"Alright. Listen, Kyree. First, I want you to kill all that 'yes, sir' shit you on. I'ma nigga just like you, and ain't nothing special about me. As long as my wife fucks with you on this business level, you good with the family. We clear on that?"

"No doubt."

"Good," Dante said. "Alright, young'n. This what I want you to do: I'ma send some niggas over to you. I want you to move in the nigga Fish Man direction and bring his ass to me. We clear?"

"Not a problem, boss man."

Hearing Dante hang up the phone, Kyree handed the phone back to his sister, with a smile on his face.

* * *

"What are you up to, Dante?" Alinna asked as soon as Dante hung up the phone with Kyree, watching and listening to him the whole phone call.

"You still dealing with them Haitians?" Dante asked without answering Alinna's question.

"Yes, Dante," she replied, catching the fact that Dante had ignored her question. "You want me to call Zoe Papi?"

"Zoe who?" Dante asked. "What happened to that other Haitian dude? Never mind. Go ahead and call him. Send a team of Haitians to Kyree for backup."

Wondering what Dante was up to, Alinna went ahead and made the call to Zoe Papi just as Monica's sister's phone started to ring.

"I got it!" Dante told Alinna, walking past her over to the bedside table, where he picked up the cell phone. "I'm listening."

"I figured out who's behind the investigation on Saldana," Monica told Dante after hearing him answer the phone. "It's not the DEA, but you was right. It's the FBI that's behind Saldana's investigation. The good news is that it has nothing to do with you. It's about the murder of known drug lord Victor Fayman and many other things the FBI has been investigating on him."

Quiet a moment, Dante stood thinking before finally saying, "Alright, Monica. I'll be in touch."

"What about my sister?" Monica asked him.

"I'll be in touch!" Dante repeated, hanging up the phone.

"What she say?" Alinna asked, drawing Dante out of his thoughts and placing his attention on her.

"From what Monica say, it's not the DEA that's trailing Dominic. It's the FBI."

"So what are you planning?" Alinna asked, seeing the look on his face.

Staring at her but not really seeing her because he was too deep in thought, he focused and said, "I wanna talk to Carmen before I decide anything."

Dante left the bedroom, leaving Alinna to her ringing cell phone. He walked to the other side of the mansion to Carmen's quarters and knocked twice on her bedroom door.

"Are you looking for me, Dante?" Carmen asked as she was walking up the hallway, heading to her bedroom.

Looking to his left and seeing Carmen, Dante turned and said, "I wanna talk to you, Carmen."

"What is it, sweetheart?" she asked, opening her bedroom door and waving him inside, only for Dante to gently grab her hand. He stopped her and asked, "Could we talk in the office in the library?"

Smiling and nodding her head, Carmen allowed Dante to lead her from her bedroom to the library. She followed him into the well-put-together office.

"Let's sit here," Dante suggested, motioning to the black fur couch across the office, against the wall.

Sitting down beside Dante, Carmen turned toward him a little and asked, "So what do you want to talk to me about, Dante?"

"Carmen, I need you to be honest with me about something."

"Dante . . . I'm always honest with you. What is this about?"

"Is there a problem going on between Dominic and the other members of the Council's Covenant? What are the other bosses talking about with Dominic having Victor Fayman?"

Staring at Dante a moment and holding his beautiful eyes, Carmen sighed softly and then said, "I won't ask how you know about Victor . . . but yes. The Council isn't happy with Dominic's decision with Victor and has expelled him from the Council."

"So basically what you're saying is that the Council is against Dominic and is turning its back on him, right?" Dante asked. Before she could say anything, he continued, "That's why the FBI is on him, or is it that the FBI is trying to get Dominic to work for them, and if I'm correct, you're back down here not only to see me but because Dominic wanted you far away from what was about to happen. Am I right, Carmen?"

Slowly smiling at Dante, Carmen reached out and laid the palm of her right hand up against the side of Dante's face and said, "You know, Dante. From the first time I saw you, I knew that you were special and extremely smart. I'm overly happy that Natalie has you in her life, but to answer your question, yes, you're right, Dante. You're right on every point you made, but now I have to ask you to help Dominic, even though he turned his back on you when you were arrested. Understand that I'm not asking you to do this for Dominic. I'm asking you to do this for me, Dante. Will you do as I ask, please?"

Dante slowly shook his head while holding Carmen's eyes. He sighed deeply and then said, "What do you want me to do, Carmen? How can I help?"

17

Dante had a long talk with Alinna after talking with Carmen for a little over two hours. He listened to her plan and actually agreed with it. Dante then broke down everything to Alinna, but added a few small ideas of his own.

"So the trip out to Puerto Rico is being put on hold, right?" Alinna asked Dante once he was finished explaining everything to her.

"For the moment . . . yes!" he answered. "But before we leave for Phoenix, I want you to contact a few people and set up a meeting. I want the family to also meet and discuss something."

"I'll take care of all that, but one more question," Alinna told him. "What about Monica? I spoke with Greg Wilson, and he say that Monica is back with the DEA."

"That may just be a good thing," Dante replied, but then said, "Call Papi Zoe or Zoe Papi . . . whatever the fuck his name is. Tell Playboy we're meeting tonight at this new club that Tony T was talking about. Also call the head of the rest of the teams that are buying work from the family. Have all of them meet us tonight at the club. Where's the cell phone that Monica calls on?"

Walking over to the bedside dresser, Alinna grabbed Monica's sister's cell phone from inside the drawer. She walked back over to Dante, handed it to him, and asked, "Are you planning on letting me know what's going on?"

"Pretty much," he answered while sliding the phone into his pocket and leaving the bedroom in search of Natalie.

Watching Dante leave the bedroom, Alinna shook her head as she walked over to her dresser, picked up her phone, and began making the calls that Dante had asked her to.

Alinna called Zoe Papi first and let him know about the meeting at Club Hypnotic. Alinna then made three more calls to her people, passing along the message about the meeting. She was just hanging up the phone, when it rang again.

"Yeah, Kyree?" Alinna answered the phone, seeing his name on the screen.

"Alinna, what's up? Dante with you?"

"No. What you need, Kyree?"

"He had me handle something and . . ."

"Did you find Fish Man or not, Kyree?"

"That's just it, Alinna! I rode out over to this nigga spot, and the shit was shut down. There wasn't nobody there. But this smoker that was hanging around the spot told me that Fish Man and like four other niggas left in a black Escalade about ten minutes before me and the team showed up."

"Alright, Kyree. I'ma let Dante know what you say, but keep watch out for both Fish Man and Rob. Call me directly if you see either of them. You understand?"

"You sounding like that nigga Dante, but I got you, boss lady."

Hanging up the phone, Alinna left the bedroom to find Vanessa.

* * *

Dante was seated inside the entertainment room, smoking a Black and shooting pool while Alinna stood at the other end talking on the phone with one of the twins. Dante lifted his eyes and saw Dre, Vanessa, Tony T, Amber, Wesley, and Harmony all walk into the room.

"What up, fam?" Tony T spoke first as he walked over to the wall where the pool sticks were lined up. "What's this meet all about?"

Dante ignored the fact that Tony T was now messing up the pool game he was in the middle of as he began racking up the balls. So Dante instead addressed the family: "What's up, family? I won't make this too long, since there's a lot going on that's being handled. I've already spoken with Alinna and Natalie. But the reason I called this meeting is to explain about what's happening tonight at Club Hypnotic with the rest of the heads from the other families working with our business. But before I go into explaining that, me and Alinna want to know how each of you feel about the family expanding business not just in Florida, but also out of the state as well."

"Out of state? Where, Dante?" Vanessa asked from over against the wall near Dre.

"Phoenix!" Alinna answered, speaking up from across the room.

"Who!" Dre said, holding up his right hand to stop the conversation. "D . . . don't ya soon-to-be father-in-law run that shit up there in Phoenix?"

Taking his turn at making a shot at the table after Tony T missed, Dante began explaining. He first started talking about the Council's Covenant, which consisted of four drug bosses that ran different parts of Arizona and other locations. He continued about Dominic once holding a seat with the Council until his decision to go up against and then murder one of the four bosses. After he was ousted from his position, there were only two remaining bosses.

"What exactly are you planning, Dante?" Vanessa asked, knowing Dante well enough to know that he wasn't telling them everything.

Meeting and holding Vanessa's eyes, Dante said, "I'm taking Dominic's position with the Council's Covenant."

"And you really think you'll be allowed to sit in one of those seats with those guys, Dante?" Harmony asked.

"Who said anything about me sitting in one of their seats?" Dante responded, smirking at Harmony. He then nodded his head at Alinna and said, "Alinna will be taking a Council seat."

"Wait a minute!" Amber said with a confused look on her face. "You just said that you're taking this Dominic guy's spot on this Council Covenant, but now you're saying that Alinna will take control of the seat or position. Explain that better, Dante."

"Maybe I can explain it better," Carmen said, drawing everyone's attention as she and Natalie entered the room. She walked over to stand beside Dante and then began to address the others: "I will be speaking on behalf of Dante to the members of the Council. I was the reason Dominic was in the position he was in while still with the Council's Covenant. My father was the founder of the Council Covenant, and after he died, the head position was left to me, but by that time I was married and Natalie had been born. I had Dominic placed in my position. But by his violation of murder of a council member, he was then automatically expelled from the Covenant."

"So you're going to put Dante . . . I mean Alinna . . . in the open seat?" Vanessa asked.

Dre added, "You really think these dudes gonna let Alinna, who's an outsider, just come and take up a position in their group?"

"Well, first, I've been thinking of having Dante and Alinna take over the two open seats. Alinna is well-educated in her field, and from what I've witnessed, she is queenpin/drug lord by right. And as for Dante, he is an extremely smart young man, and he has a very sharp and quick mind. I trust his judgment and his decision-making. With both Alinna and Dante on the Council, I'm sure things will change for the better," Carmen broke down, explaining to the family.

"You still haven't answered my question," Dre told Carmen. "What makes you think the last two members will accept Dante and Alinna into their little group?"

Slowly smiling at Dre, Carmen looked to Dante and met his eyes. She then said, "I trust that Dante knows how to change their minds very easily and quickly."

*   *   *

Dante finished up the family meeting a little bit later. He expressed to the family that both Dre and Vanessa would be taking control over things in Miami, with backup from Amber and Wesley. He, Alinna, Harmony, and Tony T would head to Phoenix.

Pulling both Dre and Vanessa to the side with him and Alinna, Dante explained that they both would be at the meeting tonight at Club Hypnotic when he announced to the heads of the other families that while he and Alinna were away, both Dre and Vanessa would take control of the family.

"Dante, can I talk to you?" Natalie asked, walking up beside him.

"What's up, beautiful?" Dante asked as he and Natalie left the others and ended up outside walking the grounds.

"Dante, I understand you're dealing with a lot of things right now, and I won't get in your way . . . but what about us?" Natalie asked, lifting her head to look up into his eyes. "You've set plans for everything, but what about you and me getting married? We can have a wedding some other time, but I want to be your wife, Dante. We can fly in my jet to the Dominican Republic tonight and be back before we have to fly to Phoenix tomorrow."

Seeing the look on Natalie's face but also thinking about the time line he was playing with flying all over the place, Dante looked back down into her hopeful eyes. He sighed deeply and said, "Alright, Natalie. We can leave after the meeting tonight at the club."

Natalie jumped up and screamed. She then wrapped her arms around Dante's neck, kissed him on the lips, and then said, "Dante, I love you so much."

* * *

Dressed alike, Dante wore a Kenneth Cole suit and white button-up with no tie, while Alinna wore a black and light gray Dolce & Gabbana full-length dress that hugged her frame perfectly. It showed off her perky breasts pressed in the top. Alinna led Dante from their bedroom, and downstairs, where Natalie, Dre, and Vanessa were all waiting and talking inside the den.

"Where's everybody?" Dante asked as he and Alinna entered the den together.

"Tony T and the others went ahead to the club," Vanessa answered, with Natalie adding, "Mother asked me to let you know that she would see us once we arrive in Phoenix tomorrow. My father sent a jet for her a few hours ago."

Nodding his head in understanding, Dante turned and started toward the front door, with both Alinna and Natalie right with him while Dre and Vanessa trailed behind them.

"We ready to roll?" James asked as soon as Dante stepped out onto the front porch sitting area, where he and Gomez stood talking.

"Yeah," Dante replied, touching his fist with James's and nodding to Gomez, who was now standing next to Natalie.

Following James out to the stretch Mercedes-Benz truck limousine, Dante nodded to Alinna's armed personal driver, who stood holding open the back door. He stepped to the side, allowing Alinna, Natalie, and then Vanessa to climb inside the limo before he and Dre got in behind the ladies.

"Dante, where are Gomez and James going?" Natalie asked once both bodyguards walked off after James closed the back door to the limo.

"They're going to follow with security, Natalie," Alinna answered as she pulled out her ringing cell phone from inside her bag, only to see Greg Wilson calling. "Yeah, Greg."

"Good evening, Mrs. Blackwell. I'm calling to let you know that I was able to get in contact with a very close friend of mine in Phoenix. I've already spoken to the person about you and Mr. Blackwell, and they'll be waiting to hear from you all."

"Tell me about him, Greg."

"It's a she, Mrs. Blackwell."

Looking at Dante as he sat talking to Natalie, Alinna focused back on the phone call. "Greg, listen to me clearly. Tell whoever this friend is that she deals with me . . . and me alone, at all times. Are we clear, Greg?"

"I'll tell Reed what you said," Greg told Alinna. "Do you want me to have her call you?"

"Yes. That's a good idea," Alinna agreed before hanging up the phone.

"You plan on telling me about that phone call?" Dante whispered over into Alinna's ear as soon as she hung up her phone.

Turning her head and meeting Dante's eyes, Alinna simply answered, "There's nothing to explain, Dante. Period!"

Nodding his head and smirking, Dante said nothing more as he pulled out his cell phone, sent a text message, and then slid the phone back into his pocket.

*　　*　　*

They pulled up onto the strip along South Beach and watched the crowd as the limousine pulled up in front of Club Hypnotic. They were surprised at how huge the crowd was, stretching two blocks and still growing. Dante spotted Tony T and Wesley as soon as they walked out the front doors of the club.

Climbing from the limousine once the back door was opened, Dante met both Tony T and Wesley as both brothers walked up.

"What's up, fam?" Tony T said, embracing Dante. As soon as Dante and Wesley embraced, Tony T continued, "Both the Haitians and the Hispanics are here already. I got 'em up in the owner's box."

"Dante," Alinna called out, touching him on his arm to get his attention. "We've got guests."

Looking in the direction suggested by Alinna, Dante stood staring at the two Range Rovers and the BMW that was between both Range Rovers just pulling up. He looked at Wesley and heard the brother say, "Relax brethren . . . Them the Rastaman there."

Shifting his attention back to the two Range Rovers and the BMW just as a slim, dark-skinned Jamaican with waist-length dreads climbed out of the back of the car, Dante whispered over to Alinna, "Why didn't you mention you brought on Jamaicans with the family?"

"It . . ." Alinna was unable to finish her sentence, as Dante walked off with Wesley, Dre, and Tony T to meet Rafael, the head of the Jamaican family. Alinna noticed his facial expression, only to hear Vanessa ask, "Alinna, what's wrong with Dante?"

"Nothing," Alinna answered, staring at Dante a moment before turning to start toward the front door. "Come on, ladies. Let's get inside."

They entered the club with no problems at all, since their people were manning the front door. Alinna led her girls into the loud and completely packed nightclub, with people everywhere, standing shoulder to shoulder.

"This is nice, Alinna," Natalie yelled over the music and bass, looking around and smiling.

"Yeah, it is . . ."

"Damn! What do we have here?" a dark-skinned guy yelled as he and two other guys walked up on Alinna, Natalie, and Vanessa. "Please tell me you three ain't here with nobody."

"Move on, homeboy," James said as he appeared out of nowhere, stepping between Alinna and the other two while facing the three guys.

"Who the fuck is you, white boy?" the dark-skinned guy asked, looking James over with a disrespectful smile on his face.

"Last time! Move on!" James repeated, staring at the guy.

"Get the fuck outta here," the guy said as he went to push James out of the way, only to find his arm bent backward, causing a scream to rip from his throat.

Watching as both friends rushed at James, Alinna slowly smiled as James connected one kick to one friend's face, sending him stumbling backward, only to follow up with a roundhouse kick that sent the other stumbling into Gomez's fist, which immediately dropped the guy out cold.

Alinna was very impressed at how quickly her security responded, swarming around her and the other ladies. Other security rushed over to help James and Gomez when the three men caused the scene. Alinna smiled at James as he walked up on her and the others, and then said, "You almost reminded me of your boy Dante just now. Where'd you come from?"

"Look!" James told her, nodding his head behind Alinna, Natalie, and Vanessa.

Alinna was not surprised to see Dante a few feet away when she turned around to see what James was talking about. She met his eyes a moment until Dante nodded his head and motioned her and the others over as he began walking through the packed club.

Catching up with Dante and seeing both Tony T and Dre with him, Alinna took Dante's hand in hers, causing him to look down to meet her eyes. He winked at her after a second, which caused her to smile.

Once they were upstairs and entered the owner's box, Tony T pulled Dante back out into the hall and nodded for his brother to follow him. He led him two doors down the hall to a room with a sign that read "Owner" on the door.

He knocked twice and then opened the door. As they walked into the office, they saw Curtis seated behind his desk talking on the phone. Tony T looked back toward Dante as his brother walked up beside him.

"Dante Blackwell," Curtis called out, smiling as he hung up his desk phone and quickly standing up from behind the desk. He walked over to Dante with his hand out for a handshake.

"Dante, this is the white guy I told you about," Tony T started. "Curtis Michael."

"Please . . . Let's all sit and talk," Curtis said, motioning for Dante and Tony T to have a seat on the couch across the office, against the wall.

"We can't stay long, Curtis," Tony T told the business owner as the three of them all sat down. "Dante still has to meet with some business friends down the hall."

"I'll make this fast then," Curtis began. "Mr. Blackwell, I'll tell you like I've told Tony T. I understand what's being said about you and your family, as you are all known. But I honestly thank you for giving me this chance with this business. There may be bad things being said about the family, but I've heard even greater things about all of you . . . and if there is anything I can do for the family in any way, please let me know."

"I'll keep that in mind," Dante told him before continuing, "I'm not sure if Tony T informed you, but in a few hours, a few of the members of the family and I will be leaving the state on business for a little while. Tony T will introduce you to Andre and Vanessa. They will be filling in for me and my wife, Alinna, until we return."

"Will Tony T be leaving as well?" Curtis asked, looking over at Tony T and then back to Dante.

"He'll be back and forth between the states. But if you need to reach Tony T or myself, just let Andre or Vanessa know. They will let us know, and we will contact you," Dante explained, watching the business partner nodding his head in understanding.

* * *

Dante left Curtis Michael's office with Tony T and walked back to the owner's box. As they walked inside, the room immediately went silent, and each of the faces inside the room turned to stare at him.

Walking around to the head of the table where Alinna was seated, Dante shook his head when Alinna started to stand. He sat inside the open seat beside her at the end of the table with six chairs.

"Where's Natalie?" Dante softly asked Alinna.

"She's with Amber and Harmony in the VIP room," Alinna told him, adding, "Both James and Gomez are with her."

Nodding his head in response, Dante said, "Continue what you were just discussing with the group."

Nodding her head, Alinna turned back to the group and continued, "As I was saying before Dante walked in the room, business will continue as is. But as of tonight and until further notice, Dre and Vanessa will be running the Blackwell family."

Alinna continued making her points to the group, even as she noticed Dante stand up and walk around the table over to the floor-to-ceiling window that overlooked the club below. She made sure each of the heads of each family knew that if anyone of them needed to contact her and Dante, they could let Dre or Vanessa know, and they would get in touch with them.

"Dante!" Alinna called out to him.

"I'm listening," he replied while still staring out the window.

"You have anything you want to add to what I've been talking about?" she asked.

Slowly shaking his head, Dante turned back to face the group and said, "Alinna explained everything. She's the head of the Blackwell family business, so I have nothing to say on what she's already discussed. Her word is law . . . but I do have something to add on a different subject. This is for everyone in this room. Let it be known that I'm putting up $50,000 each on the whereabouts of Rob Bell and the out-of-towner called Fish Man. The money will be upon delivery."

Dante noticed a few phones being pulled out as he looked back toward Alinna and nodded his head. He was just about to turn around and look out the window again, when the door opened and Wesley and Tony T walked in . . . followed by Monica.

Dante looked at both Wesley and Tony T, and then nodded for both of them to leave. He then motioned Monica over to him just as Alinna hopped up from her seat, which caused Vanessa to jump up as well. Both women rushed over and stood in front of Dante, with burners already gripped tightly in their hands.

"What the fuck are you doing here?" Alinna asked, sounding more like she was growling out her words.

"Alinna, relax . . . ," Dante told her as he then looked over at Vanessa and said, "Take Alinna back to her seat."

Looking back at Dante and meeting his eyes for a few seconds, Vanessa sighed and grabbed Alinna's hand, forcefully pulling her out of the way.

"Why the hell did you call me here?" Monica asked with an attitude before turning her angry stare from Alinna over to meet Dante's eyes.

"This meeting is over," Dante called out, dismissing everyone from the room while holding Monica's stare.

After the others left the room, Alinna and Vanessa stared hard at Monica. Dante ignored both of them, instead speaking directly to Monica: "Last time we met was inside of a nightclub this same way. You offered two choices that time, and I chose one."

"What the hell are you getting at, Dante?" Monica asked nastily.

"I'm offering you two choices now," Dante explained, using a calm voice while still locking eyes with her. "I know you're back with the DEA, so you can either get a transfer from the Miami office and move out to Phoenix and work for me, or I can erase you and your whole family from this world. And I mean your grandmother and father who live in Sterling Heights, Michigan. Also, your Godmother and her three middle-aged kids who live in Salt Lake City. I also know about your best friend, Sherry Williams, whose house you was hiding at down south. So tell me, Agent Monica Martin. What's your decision?"

* * *

"You wanna tell me how the hell you knew all that stuff about her family?" Alinna asked as soon as Vanessa escorted Monica from the owner's box. She continued before Dante could respond, "And when the fuck was you planning on telling me you decided on taking this bitch with us to Phoenix, Dante?"

"You finish yet?" he asked Alinna in a calm voice.

"Nigga . . . don't play with me!" Alinna said, walking up in Dante's face. "You better answer my question, or I promise you, we will be tearing this shit up in here, Dante. Please don't play with me."

"Relax, Alinna," Dante answered, stepping around her to walk away, only for Alinna to grab his arm and snatch him back around to face her.

"Where the fuck are you going?" Alinna demanded. "We're not finished talking yet."

Sighing, Dante said, "Alinna, look . . . You'll get a call later tonight from someone naked Kerri Cook. She's a friend of mine, and I hired her to be your assistant. She'll explain everything to you."

"Who is she, Dante?" Alinna asked, stopping him from walking away again.

"She's the same person that helped me out while I was locked up. How the hell you think I was getting shit done? Who you think help Vanessa and them set up Geno so Vanessa could kidnap Geno and get Mya for me? Look, Alinna . . . I know we've had our trouble with women in our past, but other than Natalie, I never wanted anything to do with Angela. But if you can't trust me enough to know that whatever I do, I do for you—for us—then what's the point of us being together? I love you, but I gotta go. I'ma call you from the jet."

Watching Dante turn and walk out of the owner's box, Alinna turned and walked over to the window overlooking the VIP section. She looked out just as Dante walked into the section. She then saw Natalie rush over to him, throw her arms around his neck for a hug, and then kiss him.

Looking down as she held up her ring hand, and staring at the diamond that Dante had given to her, Alinna lifted her eyes just in time to see both Dante and Natalie leaving the VIP room, already knowing where the two of them were headed.

18

The feeling of her neck being kissed and her left breast gently squeezed woke Alinna from her sleep. She rolled over to her right and blinked her eyes a few times to clear her vision. She found herself staring at Dante, who was smirking right back at her.

"You miss me, shorty?" Dante softly asked, bending down to kiss Alinna's lips before shifting himself until he was lying between her legs and leaning over her.

"What time is it?" Alinna asked as she felt Dante pushing her panties to the side.

"It's almost 5:00 a.m.," Dante told her as he led his manhood inside of her. Her soft moans put a smile on his face.

Losing all train of thought as Dante began moving in and out of her, Alinna pushed back against him as he pushed deeper inside of her. She felt herself quickly getting close to cumming. She wrapped her arms tight around his neck, pulled his head down until their lips touched, and then kissed him.

"Oh God . . . Dante!" Alinna cried, breaking their kiss. "Dante, I'm cumming. Baby, I'm cumming!"

Continuing to make love to Alinna, and watching her face as he brought her to orgasm after orgasm, Dante finally released himself deep inside her, feeling the muscles inside her working him . . . milking him . . . as she held him tightly against her chest.

Alinna then rolled over to her right and faced Dante once he pulled out of her and lay beside her. She then laid her head on his chest. For just a few moments, they lay there together quietly until Dante spoke up, "I'm sorry about what happened before I left the club with Natalie. You was right.

I was supposed to tell you about my decisions before I put them into play. I'm sorry."

"I'm sorry too," Alinna told him, sitting up and staring down into Dante's eyes. "You was right also, baby. I need to trust you and not question you when you do make a decision. It won't happen again. I promise."

Leaning up to kiss her, Dante then said, "What time we leaving?"

"In another two hours," Alinna answered, but then asked, "Did you and Natalie get that taken care of?"

"Yeah. We got married, and she has the paperwork with her."

"So why aren't you with her, Dante?"

"She's asleep, and I wanted to see you."

Smiling at his answer, Alinna said, "I missed you too, Dante. But don't let her wake up and you're not with her. She should wake up next to her husband."

"What about you?"

"I'm always there when you need me. I love you, Dante."

Staring up at Alinna a moment, Dante asked, "Why, Alinna?"

"Why what?" she responded, staring back at Dante as he gave her a look without answering her question. She sighed deeply and then said, "Because I love you, Dante. I know everything I've put you through . . . and you're still here with me. I understand that everything you've done is for us, and all I've ever done was trip out because of Angela, when I should have trusted you and known that I was the one you loved. Even now with how you feel for Natalie. I know you love her, but I know that in the end it's me that holds your heart. Natalie also has a place in it now, and I won't hurt you again or push you away. So if allowing Natalie into our family is what it takes, I'm willing to deal with it."

Still staring at Alinna, Dante said, "What are we going to do about the sleeping arrangement?"

Understanding perfectly what Dante was really asking her, Alinna sighed deeply again and then said, "Our closet is big enough for her things, Dante, and our bed is big enough for the three of us."

"I'm glad you said that, since Natalie already set up where we going to be staying at in Phoenix," Dante told Alinna. "She spoke with a real estate agent, and Carmen already took care of payments on the house."

Shaking her head and unable to stop from smiling, Alinna rolled away from Dante to her left, climbed out of bed, and started toward the bathroom. Over her shoulder, she looked back at Dante and said, "Come on so we can shower and you can get back to Natalie before she gets up."

* * *

Alinna's bags were packed, and she was dressed and ready to go by the time Dante and Tony T finally came downstairs with Dre. Alinna waited as the guys talked about last-minute plans. Alinna sat beside Vanessa, Amber, and Harmony, with Mya sitting next to her and D.J. on her lap.

"Ya'll ready?" Dante asked as he, Dre, and Tony T walked into the den. He looked around and then asked, "Where's Natalie?"

"She left with Gomez to handle something," Alinna told Dante as she bent forward to kiss D.J. goodbye on his cheek.

"Where the hell she went, Alinna?" Dante asked as both D.J. and Mya ran over to him for a hug.

"Dante, relax! Natalie is meeting us at the jet," Alinna explained. "She said she wanted to take care of something before we left."

Dante didn't respond as he sat down next to Mya. He then reached over and dapped up with Dre's son—his nephew and godson, A.J. He then looked over at Harmony and asked, "You alright, baby girl?"

"I'm fine, boo," Harmony answered, smiling at Dante.

"The bag's already inside the truck," Alinna told Dante as they started walking to the front door. "We'll take the Phantom. Natalie has your Bentley."

Once outside, Dante said a few more words to Dre and hugged a crying Vanessa. He then hugged Mya and D.J. again, and even A.J., only to end up dealing with a crying Amber hugging him.

"What's up with all this crying?" Tony T asked everybody. "We not staying up there. This still home right here."

"Shut up, Tony T!" Amber told him, pushing Tony T upside his head. "I'ma miss my girls and my brother, Dante."

"Oh, so you not going to miss me too?" Tony T asked playfully.

"Shut up, boy!" Amber told him again, rolling her eyes.

"Amber . . . where my nigga Wesley at?" Dante asked at the thought of his brother.

"You know Wesley, Dante. He been gone since 5:30 this morning," Amber told Dante. "Yeah, also . . . Wesley told me to tell you that if you need him, he would be on the first plane or jet to Phoenix."

"Where's James?" Dante asked as he was climbing in the back of the Phantom.

"He's riding with security," Alinna informed him, getting inside the Phantom behind Dante.

Leaving the mansion once Tony T and Harmony were inside the car, Dante pulled out his cell phone and texted a message. Both Harmony and Alinna were talking while Tony T was rolling a blunt. Dante waited for a reply from his text message, but then realized no return message was coming.

"Dante, you okay?" Alinna asked, watching him even while she was talking to Harmony.

"I'm good, shorty," Dante answered while sending another text message that was actually a direct warning to the receiver.

*   *   *

They arrived at the airstrip about fifteen minutes after leaving the mansion. They pulled up in front of the jet and saw the Bentley and a Chevy Malibu. Dante was the first one out of the Phantom, just as Gomez appeared at the door to the jet.

"Who's the Malibu belong to?" Tony asked, climbing out of the car.

"A friend," Dante answered as Alinna and Harmony got out next.

Dante had the team of ten security guards handle the bags as he led the others onto the jet. He barely walked completely onto the jet before he was attacked by Natalie. He had to catch his balance and catch Natalie to keep her from falling backward into Alinna and the others.

"What took you so long?" Natalie questioned him after kissing him on the lips.

"Why didn't you tell me you was leaving this morning before we left?" Dante asked, ignoring her question.

"Because I've got a surprise for you," Natalie answered, taking Dante's hand and leading him toward the back of the jet.

"Hold up, Natalie," Dante told her after seeing Kerri seated next to a window smiling at him. "What's up, Kerri? I see you made it."

"Why would I not show up?" Kerri said, standing up from her seat and hugging Dante's neck tightly.

Returning Kerri's hug but releasing her after a few seconds, Dante first introduced Natalie as his wife, and then turned to Alinna and introduced her: "Kerri, this is my wife, Alinna, and the person you'll be working with."

"I've heard a lot about you from Dante and from people on the streets," Kerri said, shaking Alinna's hand. "It's good to finally meet you."

"It's good to meet you too, Kerri," Alinna replied, smiling at the woman that Dante assigned to be her assistant. "Go ahead and relax and rest. We'll talk business once we land in Phoenix."

"Kerri . . . this for you!" Dante told her, handing her a white envelope he pulled from the inside pocket of his black leather jacket before he walked off.

"What's this?" Kerri asked, looking from the envelope to Alinna.

"Who knows what Dante's giving you," Alinna said, smiling as she stood watching Kerri open the envelope.

"Oh . . . my . . . God!" Kerri got out in shock, seeing the envelope was filled with nothing but hundreds. "Is he really serious, Alinna?"

"Dante doesn't play games, Kerri," Alinna explained before adding, "Just know that if Dante is doing this for you, it's because he actually likes you . . . and that doesn't happen very often. Welcome to the family."

*   *   *

"What's that?" Dante asked Natalie as he accepted the small gift bag she handed him while the two sat together at the back of the jet.

"It's your surprise, Dante. Open it!" Natalie insisted excitedly.

Shaking his head and smirking, Dante dug inside the bag and pulled out colored tissue paper and a small ring box. He looked over at a smiling Natalie as he opened the box to see a white gold and platinum band with white diamonds around the band.

"Do you like it?" Natalie asked, still smiling at Dante.

"Yeah! Hell yeah, beautiful!" Dante answered, leaning over to kiss her.

Natalie took the ring from Dante and then grabbed his left hand. She then held up the new ring next to the ring he was already wearing. They looked the same. Natalie then said, "It looks just like the one Alinna bought for you."

Dante allowed Natalie to slide the ring onto his finger on his right hand as he met her eyes. He kissed her, hearing her say, "I love you, Mr. Blackwell."

"I love you, too, Mrs. Blackwell," Dante answered, only to receive another kiss from her.

*   *   *

They landed in Phoenix some hours later. Dante was woken up by Harmony, with Natalie on his left side and Alinna on his right side, both asleep as well. Dante blinked a few times and focused on Tony T standing in front of him.

"Bruh, we there," Tony T announced, but then nodded toward the window and said, "We've got company."

Dante leaned forward and looked out the window. He saw a white Mercedes limousine and two Lincoln Navigators parked behind it. He recognized Dominic's suit-wearing security team that stood fifteen deep, surrounding the limo.

"What's going on?" Alinna asked as she sat forward blinking her eyes as she focused first on Tony T and then over to Dante.

"It's my mother," Natalie spoke up as she woke up and stared out the window. "I forgot to mention that she was meeting us when the jet landed."

Making their way off the jet, Dante led the group off. Upon seeing Carmen climbing out of the limousine, Natalie rushed off from beside Dante, reaching Carmen first with a big smile on her face.

Walking up to where Carmen and Natalie were standing and having a few words, Dante met Carmen's eyes once she turned her attention to him. "Hello, Carmen."

"You should really start calling me Mom now, Dante," Carmen told him, hugging her new son-in-law. "Natalie just told me you two went and got married early this morning . . . late last night."

"Look at his ring, Mother," Natalie told her, picking up Dante's right hand to show off the ring she bought for him.

Nodding her head in approval, Carmen met Dante's stare again and said, "I don't need to explain why Dominic isn't here, do I?"

"It's not necessary," Dante replied.

"Very good. Let me introduce to you our new head of security," Carmen told Dante, motioning to a blond, short-haired white man dressed in a black suit. "Justin Mitchell, meet Dante Blackwell."

"I've heard a lot about you, Mr. Blackwell," Justin said, holding out his hand for a handshake.

Ignoring the hand the man held out to him, Dante looked back at Carmen and asked, "What happened to the other head of security?"

"He quit a few days ago, but this was his replacement he brought to us," Carmen explained. "Is everything okay, Dante?"

Looking back at Justin Mitchell, Dante stood staring at the guy a moment, ignoring Natalie asking him what was wrong. He finally spoke, "Carmen, I hope you trust me, because if you're sure about placing me in a seat with the Council, then you're willing to back up each of my decisions."

"Of course, Dante!" Carmen said, barely finishing her sentence when Dante moved in what was like a blur as two guns were leveled and trained on Justin Mitchell. She stepped away from Justin and pulled Natalie with her as Dante and everyone who was with him stood staring at Justin.

"One question . . . and I expect one answer . . . which better be the truth!" Dante told the white man. "Who is it that you work for?"

"What are you . . . whoa!" Justin cried, throwing up both his hands at seeing Dante's finger on the trigger of both Glocks he was pointing at him. "Relax, man. I'll answer your questions."

"You've got five seconds to start talking . . . and you're already down to three. Talk!"

Seeing the dangerously serious look on Dante Blackwell's face, Justin swallowed the lump that formed inside his throat before saying, "I work for Fredrick Roosevelt. He set it up for me to come over and spy on Dominic Saldana."

Seeing Dante's eyes shift over to her a moment before focusing back on Justin, Carmen understood the look and explained, "Fredrick Roosevelt is one of the remaining members of the Council. He runs most of the northwest area of Arizona and a little of the southwest area as well, Dante."

"James," Dante called while staring directly into Justin's eyes.

"What's up, bruh?" James said as he slid up beside Dante on his left side.

"Take our friend Justin, here, and watch him," Dante told James while holstering both his burners. "I'll deal with him later."

"Dante, how did you know that he worked for Roosevelt? What gave it away?" Carmen asked as she motioned him and the others over to the limousine.

"His eyes!" Dante told Carmen, motioning for both her and Natalie to climb inside the limo. He then allowed both Alinna and Harmony to climb inside next. Kerri followed, with Tony T last.

"Dante, I don't understand," Carmen told him once everyone was inside the limousine. "You said that you could tell he worked for someone else just by his eyes. How is that so?"

"It's just something my father taught me when I was young," Dante explained, but quickly changed the subject asking, "Where's Dominic now?"

"He had a business meeting earlier, but he should be back at the mansion now. Why?"

"I want to speak with him. But tell me something. What time is the meeting set with the Council?"

"Actually, Dante, I informed both Fredrick and Samuel Atlas that there will be a meeting tomorrow evening. Why do you ask?"

"Change the time," Dante told Carmen, pulling out his cell phone to see he had a text message. While opening and reading the message, he continued, "Set the meeting for two hours."

"Today?" Carmen asked, staring at Dante.

"Pretty much!" Dante responded just as he finished typing out a text message.

Dante knew that Carmen would have to deal with both Roosevelt and Atlas complaining about the sudden change for the meeting. Carmen pulled out her phone and was just beginning to dial a number, when Dante spoke up again, "By the way, Carmen, from now on, Tony T will be the new head of security for us."

"Of course, Dante," Carmen said, smiling as she cut her eyes over in Dante's direction, loving the take-charge attitude and leadership he displayed.

* * *

"This supposed to be our new house you was telling me about?" Alinna asked, leaning over toward Dante as she stared out the limo's window, watching as they drove up a long drive, only to turn off in front of a huge mansion.

"Actually . . . ," Natalie said, leaning forward beside Dante to look over to Alinna. "This is my mother and father's house. We will be staying in Scottsdale. That's actually in the southwest area and east of Phoenix. It's kind of like the country a little, but it's nice. You'll like it, Alinna."

Once the limousine pulled to a stop in front of the mansion, and the door was opened by the armed driver, Carmen was first to step out, followed by Natalie and the others.

"This is nice," Harmony said as she stood looking around the place.

"Why don't all of you come with me," Carmen spoke up, motioning for everyone to follow her. "I'll show everyone around while Dante speaks with my husband. You do remember where to find Dominic, right Dante?"

"I'll see you guys in a minute," Dante said, first kissing Alinna and then Natalie before turning and walking up the steps to the front door, where the butler stood holding open the door.

"Welcome back, Mr. Blackwell," the butler told Dante with a welcoming smile as Dante walked past him, nodded his response, and entered the mansion.

Inside the mansion, Dante headed straight to Dominic's office. He knocked twice, opened the door, and walked in, catching Dominic talking on his phone seated behind his desk.

Watching Dominic's eyes widen and his expression quickly change once he looked up and locked eyes with him, Dante continued watching. Dominic's expression quickly turned from surprise and fear to anger.

"What the hell are you doing in my house?" Dominic yelled angrily, slamming down the telephone and staring hard directly at Dante.

Ignoring the yelling and even the mean-mugging, Dante calmly closed the office door behind him and then walked over to the two-cushioned couch in front of Dominic's desk. He sat down but continued to stare straight back at the Dominican drug lord.

"You plan on answering my question or just sitting there staring at me like you've forgotten how to speak?" Dominic asked with much anger.

"I'm actually reminding myself why I haven't ended your worthless life already!" Dante told the drug lord with a calm and coldness that caused Dominic to sit back with fear easily noticeable on his face. "I won't discuss what you did to my family while I was locked up and how you treated Natalie when she decided to come to Miami to support me. This visit to Phoenix this time is at the request of your wife, Carmen . . ."

"What the hell does . . . !"

"As of right now, you will give up you connects as well as your buyers!" Dante continued after being cut off, only to cut Dominic back off. "I'm fully aware that you're no longer on the Council's seat. I will be taking over that position as well. Also, from this very moment, Carmen will now have full control over the money, businesses, this house, and even the cars. She has full control of everything, and this isn't a request. Now tell me . . . when did you notice the FBI was watching you?"

"Who the hell do you think you are?" Dominic yelled, jumping up from his desk chair and pointing his finger at Dante. "You storm into my office demanding that I tell you my connects and my buyers . . . and demanding that I give full control of everything I own over to my wife. Have you lost your fucking mind?"

"Sit down, Dominic," Dante calmly told the drug lord.

"Get the hell out . . . !"

"Sit the fuck down, Dominic!" Dante repeated a little more forcefully while opening his leather jacket and showing both his bangers. "I won't ask again."

Staring at Dante a moment, Dominic slowly sat down behind his desk, allowing thoughts of going for the .38 revolver that was inside his top desk drawer, but he quickly gave up on the thought, remembering exactly what the young man seated in front of him was capable of doing to a person.

19

Meeting with both Alinna and Natalie in the guest house, in which he once lived, Dante caught both women in the middle of a conversation while seated at the breakfast counter drinking a pink drink. Alinna saw him walk through the front door first.

"How'd the meeting go with Dominic?" Alinna asked Dante as he walked up between the two women at the breakfast bar.

"Alright," Dante answered, taking Alinna's glass of fruit juice from the counter and taking a drink. After setting the glass back down, he asked, "Where are the others?"

"Carmen took Tony T to meet the other security team and introduce him. Harmony went with 'im just to look around the place some more," Alinna explained.

"Baby, I was thinking," Natalie spoke up. "If you're making Tony T the head of security, he should be close to mother and father, right?"

"Carmen's my concern, but you're right!" Dante agreed, catching the quick flash of sadness that shot across Natalie's face before she spoke up again.

"I'm going to call my real estate agent and have her find a place for Tony T and Harmony close to here, but they can stay here in the guest house until everything is settled. What do you think?" Natalie asked, smiling at Dante.

"Handle it!" Dante told Natalie, who then looked over to Alinna and asked, "Where's Kerri at?"

"Talking with the real estate agent!" Alinna told Dante with a grin, nodding toward the back door that led out to the pool.

Shaking his head and smirking, Dante said, "Well, since you two got all that figured out, can we get something to eat now? We never did get breakfast."

"We can go to Antonio's," Natalie told Dante, standing up from her seat at the counter. "They serve lunch and dinner, and Mari owns the place."

"I'm with it!" Dante agreed as Alinna stood up beside him.

"Who's Mari?" Alinna asked Dante in a lowered voice.

"Mari is Natalie's best friend . . . and also has a thing for James," Dante told her, smirking at the thought of James and Mari.

*   *   *

Dante had lunch with Natalie, Alinna, James, and Kerri, and he met Mari again, who was more excited to see him than he expected her to be. He then introduced both Alinna and Kerri to Mari, and then sat back and watched James play it cool as Mari boldly and openly flirted with the bodyguard.

They spent longer than they expected at the restaurant, leaving once Carmen called and explained that it was time for the meeting. Natalie agreed for everyone that they would all go out sometime soon.

Back inside Dante's old Benz that Carmen and Dominic gave to him when he first agreed to work for Dominic, Dante gave James the address to where the meeting would be held. But he then looked back to Alinna, hearing her ask, "So what are you planning, Dante?"

"This is basically our introduction to the Council's remaining two members, and then we're going to establish our position," Dante broke down, explaining to the others.

"Establish . . . huh?" Alinna said, smirking at Dante from her seat in the back.

Winking his eyes at her and smirking, Dante turned back around in his front seat to allow himself some thinking time before they reached the meeting location.

*   *   *

Staring out the back window of the Mercedes up at the tall building made mostly of straight glass, Alinna waited until James parked the Benz and Dante opened her door for her. She then climbed out from the car and looked up at the building.

"Let's get this over with," Dante said, leading the others through the front entrance of the building.

Alinna noticed the security as soon as they entered the building, but she continued to follow Dante, who acted as if he didn't even see them or the woman who sat behind the front desk. The secretary quickly snatched up her desk phone and stared at them. Alinna looked at Natalie as both women saw the serious expression the secretary had on her face, which made Alinna smile in approval.

They took the elevator up to the fourteenth floor and then followed Dante once they got off. They noticed James shifting his position over beside her. Alinna then saw two suit-wearing white men who were posted outside of the oak wood door to which Dante was heading at the end of the hall.

"Who are you?" one of the men asked, looking Dante over before looking over at Alinna on his right.

"I'm here for the meeting, and they're with me," Dante told the guy, nodding to the others. "I'm Dante Blackwell."

Once of the suited guys pulled out a walkie-talkie announcing that Dante was there for the meeting. Alinna started to step inside the room. However, the guy immediately went to stop her from entering, with a hand against her chest.

"Only . . ."

Immediately, the one man went flying inside the office, barely noticing Dante's quick movement before his fist smashed into his throat. Alinna shifted her eyes to the right, just in time to see James connect an elbow to the second man's chest, dropping him immediately.

Smirking as she entered the office, she stepped around the suit who was laid out on the floor holding his throat and trying to breathe. Alinna instantly laid eyes on Carmen, who was seated at a long, glass, six-chair table. Carmen smiled and stared at Alinna.

"Gentlemen . . . ," Carmen spoke up, still smiling. "Allow me to introduce my son-in-law, Dante Blackwell, and his wife Alinna. You all know my daughter, Natalie, right?"

"Was any of this really necessary, Mr. Blackwell?" aa slim, middle-aged white man with long black hair in a ponytail asked while motioning to the security still lying on the floor.

"He needs to learn to keep his hands to himself when dealing with either Mrs. Blackwells," Dante stated as he followed behind Alinna and Natalie over to two open seats on each side of Carmen. He then nodded slightly to Tony T, who stood directly behind Carmen against the wall. Dante stood to the left of Carmen, staring first at the white guy who spoke up, before shifting his eyes over to the heavy-set white man wearing glasses. He stared directly at him and said, "Which one of you is Fredrick Roosevelt?"

"He is!" the ponytailed guy answered, nodding over to the heavy-set man.

Slowly nodding his head while still staring at the heavy-set white man, Dante smirked slightly. But then he began to speak: "I'm sure Carmen has already informed the both of you that since Mr. Saldana has been expelled as a member of the Council's Covenant for his violation against a fellow member of the Council due to this major issue, I will be assuming the position as head of the Council . . ."

"Now wait just a God damn minute!" Fredrick Roosevelt yelled, cutting off Dante in the middle of what he was saying. "You can't just walk in here and demand control of anything. Who the hell do you think you are?"

Dante simply glanced over at Roosevelt but ignored him. He then continued what he was saying as if Fredrick Roosevelt never spoke up: "As Carmen explained to the both of you, I'm sure, I will be filling in the seat as head. But first thing as head, I am releasing my position over to my wife, Alinna Blackwell, and I will simply become an active member . . ."

"This is bullshit!" Fredrick Roosevelt yelled, slamming his fist down onto the table. "I will not stand for this! This street thug . . . !"

"Leave!" Dante said loud enough to cut off the man.

"What did you say?" Fredrick asked, staring hard at Dante, not sure he heard him correctly.

"I said leave!" Dante repeated, but then added, "Whoever doesn't agree with the change that's happening can leave now!"

"This is complete bullshit!" Fredrick said as he sat staring hard and completely pissed off at Dante.

"Seeing that you're still sitting, I'll take it that you agree with what's happening then, Mr. Roosevelt," Dante told him, but then added, "And understand . . . that if you open your mouth one more time while anyone is speaking, you will not only leave this meeting, but you will no longer be a member of the Council."

Staring at Fredrick a moment and holding the fat man's gaze, Dante slowly shifted his eyes over to Samuel Atlas and said, "Mr. Atlas, do you agree with what's happening, or are you in disagreement with what I've just stated?"

"If Carmen wants the two of you seated as the head of the Council, I will not go against her wishes. I actually trust her judgment," Samuel told Dante as he nodded his head toward Carmen.

Shifting his head toward Carmen, he caught a small smile she allowed to show, and Dante had a quick thought. But he ignored it for the moment as he continued, "Now that we are all in agreement, I'll let Mrs. Blackwell speak with you."

Remaining in her seat and staring at the two drug lords across the table from her a few seconds, Alinna finally began, "Okay, gentlemen . . . I understand this is all new for the both of you, but I have some ideas that will not only make us more money but also build business to another level . . ."

"This is bullshit!" Fredrick Roosevelt again said in a low voice, shaking his head.

Continuing what she was saying and ignoring Roosevelt's comments, Alinna caught Dante from the corner of her eye. While she continued to speak, she followed his movement across the room.

"What is this? Get your hands off of me, you son of a bitch!" Fredrick yelled, trying to pull away from Dante, who was now dragging him from his seat toward the door.

Waiting until Dante escorted Roosevelt out of the room and was back standing at her right shoulder and to Carmen's left, Alinna started to speak. However, she paused when Mr. Atlas spoke up saying, "Excuse me, but, Carmen, where did you find Mr. Blackwell? I truly like the way he handles business, and he is truly a man of his word as seen."

Smiling proudly as she cut her eyes over to Dante, Carmen looked back to Atlas and gently said, "He is my son-in-law, Samuel."

*   *   *

"Dante . . . do you think that was a wise decision with expelling Fredrick from the Council at a time like this?" Carmen asked him as they stood together outside and in front of her limousine after the meeting was completed.

"Roosevelt's a problem, and I can see him becoming an even bigger one," Dante replied, cutting his eyes over to where Alinna and Kerri stood talking with Samuel Atlas, with James just a few feet away.

"I agree with you about Fredrick. But don't you think that, since you've not only expelled him but also humiliated him in front of everyone, maybe we now have an enemy?" Carmen asked, sounding slightly worried.

"He was already an enemy, Carmen," Dante told her. "The only difference between now and before is that instead of having the enemy on the inside, he's now on the outside trying to figure out what's going on inside."

"Are we able to handle this?" Carmen asked. "Fredrick has a great deal of power and can become a big problem, Dante."

"I'll handle it," Dante told Carmen, receiving a small smile and a nod of the head just as Samuel Atlas called to both of them waving his goodbye, "There's something you wanna tell him, Carmen?"

Looking back to Dante, Carmen said, "Maybe later. But how about telling me how you plan on filling in all the open seats on the Council, Dante?"

"I have three people in mind," Dante told her, winking his eye at his mother-in-law, which caused her to smile and shake her head.

20

Alinna was deep in thought, wondering where the hell Dante had gone off to without telling her or Natalie. However, she lost her train of thought when an excited Natalie grabbed her arm and called her name. Alinna then turned her attention to Natalie but noticed the huge mansion that Carmen's driver was pulling up to. As he stopped in front of an iron gate, Alinna noticed the brick wall that surrounded the entire estate.

"Who the hell lives here?" Alinna asked, staring out the window.

"We do!" Natalie answered her as the gate opened and the limousine pulled inside the estate.

"You gotta be joking!" Alinna mumbled as the limo pulled to a stop at what looked like the main house to the estate.

"Alinna . . . come on in!" Natalie cried excitedly, pulling her from the limo as soon as the driver opened the back door.

"How big is this place?" Alinna asked, looking around.

"It's 26,862 square feet, and we're sitting on 4.5 acres of land," Natalie told Alinna with a smile as she unlocked and opened the oil-shined, dark brown, thick wooden front door. "It's composed of four separate buildings. There's the main house . . .what we're in now. There's also the pool cabana, guest house, and a detached garage."

Following Natalie through the mansion, Alinna saw all eleven bedrooms and seventeen bathrooms, and then noticed the handcrafted wood paneling and solid walnut doors that Natalie pointed out. There were elaborate beamed and hand-painted ceilings, ancient stone floors, exotic wood-paneled walls, authentic Italian lighting, and even an imported hand-carved stone fireplace. Alinna then followed Natalie from the state-of-the-art chef-style kitchen outside, where a still excited Natalie showed her the 3,000+-square-foot pool where Carmen was talking to a middle-aged white woman.

Natalie introduced Alinna to Emmy Jones, the house servant. Alinna had a few words with the woman before Natalie was pulling her off to see the water features in the pool. While standing under the gazebo, Natalie pointed out the terraced gardens, olive orchard, and the private jogging trail that surrounded the entire estate.

"Does Dante like basketball?" Natalie asked as she and Alinna stopped at the sunken court.

"He talks about it a lot with Tony T and Dre back home," Alinna replied, staring at the nicely built basketball court.

"Well, now Dante and Tony T have some place to play sometime," Natalie said with a smile. "Let's go back to the main house."

Following alongside Natalie and listening to the other women explain more about the house, Alinna noticed James standing at the pool watching her, with Kerri alongside him. Looking around, Alinna steered Natalie in James and Kerri's direction.

"Dante's here!" James told Alinna once she and Natalie stopped in front of them.

"How long has he been here?" Alinna asked as she started toward the swinging glass doors that led back into the house.

"He just got here a few minutes ago," James told her.

Kerri then got the attention of both Alinna and Natalie and said, "I heard back from the real estate agent, and she's free to show Tony T and Harmony around a few places tomorrow. I'm going to need Tony T and Harmony's number for the agent."

"Remind me later on," Alinna told Kerri as they were entering the main house.

*   *   *

Alinna searched for Dante in the house but ran into Emmy, who told her that Carmen was at the guest house with Dante and a Ms. Martin. Alinna thanked her and started for the guest quarters, not quite believing what she just heard about Monica being at their house.

"Alinna, correct me if I'm wrong, but this Ms. Martin . . . Isn't that the same person as the DEA woman Monica Martin whose sister we're still holding?"

"That's her!" Alinna answered, face balled up in anger.

Reaching the guest house and entering without announcing or knocking, Alinna first saw Carmen seated at the bar table. Dante was standing next to her smoking a Black & Mild, when Alinna shouted, "Where the fuck is she, Dante?"

Dante was leaning against the bar too, resting on his forearm. He stared at Alinna and said, "She's in the bedroom, Alinna."

"Why the fuck is she even here?" Alinna screamed, staring fire at Dante.

"Alinna, we discussed this!" Dante calmly stated. "She's going to be working for me."

"I'm talking about in this fucking house, Dante! Don't play with me!" Alinna spit out angrily.

"Relax, Rodriguez . . . I'm only staying until I find a new place out here," Monica said, walking out into the front room from the bedroom.

Staring at Monica a moment but rolling her eyes back at Dante, she said, "You better keep this bitch on a real short leash and out of my path, or you'll find her ass dead the next time you're looking for her."

Watching as Alinna stormed out of the guest house, Natalie turned back to Dante and asked, "Why didn't you tell us you were bringing her here, Dante?"

"It was a last-minute decision, Natalie," Dante answered as he put out his Black inside the crystal ashtray.

"How long is she supposed to stay here?" Natalie asked, shooting Monica a nasty look before focusing back on Dante.

"I'ma talk with you about that later," Dante told her, but added after seeing the look she was giving him, "I need you to talk with your real estate agent and see what she can find for Monica."

"The faster you get that taken care of, the faster you won't have to see me around here," Monica added, staring at Natalie.

"Just shut the hell up!" Natalie told Monica, rolling her eyes as she turned and left the guest house.

*   *   *

"Who's the diamond princess?" Monica asked, turning and looking over at Dante after Alinna and then the young pretty Spanish woman walked out the front door of the guest house.

"Dante, I'll leave you to talk with your friend a while," Carmen said, standing up from her seat at the bar. "If I'm still here, come and see me before I leave . . . or just call me tonight."

Accepting the kiss to the cheek from Carmen, but catching the look she shot Monica on the way out the door, Dante waited until Carmen was gone, focused on Monica, and then said, "You should watch what you say. You can find yourself in trouble if you don't."

"More trouble than you already got me in? I doubt it!" Monica said, walking over and dropping into the couch that was in front of a wall-unit, 38-inch flat-screen television. "Anyway, what is the whole reason for me coming here with you?"

"When is it you're supposed to start at the new office or agency?"

"It starts tomorrow. I'm already in the system as an agent, but what exactly are you planning on having me do for you?"

"For right now, I just want you to get yourself settled in and feel yourself around. Get to know some people, and when the time comes, I'ma let you know what I need," Dante told her.

"What about my sister and brother-in-law?" Monica asked, sitting forward on the couch, staring at Dante.

"I gave you my word that once you got here, I would have your sister and brother-in-law released. But the first time you cross me, Monica, I will kill you. Are we clear?"

"You don't scare me, Dante!"

"That's good to hear," Dante replied, walking toward the front door but stopping and looking back at Monica. "We'll see about getting you some wheel's tomorrow. You holding?"

"I turned in my service gun before I left Miami. I won't have a new one until I meet with my new boss," Monica explained to him.

"I want you to have a personal one as well. We'll take care of that tomorrow, too," Dante told her, walking out the door, leaving Monica sitting on the couch.

Heading back to the main house, and passing armed security guards that Tony T had assigned to the estate, Dante stopped by the kitchen and asked Emmy for something to drink.

After being handed a bottled water, Dante said, "Emmy, you seen where Carmen or either Mrs. Blackwell went to?" he asked after taking a long sip.

"All three women are in the gazebo, Mr. Blackwell," Emmy told him, showing a small smile as she returned back to preparing dinner.

"Call me Dante, Emmy. And thanks," Dante said as he left the kitchen and went in search for his wives and mother-in-law.

*   *   *

"I don't want or like her in the same house that I'm supposed to live in . . . no matter what Dante is planning!" Alinna was saying as she, Natalie, and Carmen all sat inside the gazebo together discussing Dante bringing Monica into their new home.

"Alinna . . . ," Carmen began, drawing both younger women's attention to her. "We three all know by now how Dante is. He's a thinker. This we know. He's also an amazing planner. This we also know. But knowing these things, we also know that Dante doesn't always share his plans until he feels they're right for us to know. We may not agree with it, but can any of us say truthfully that Dante doesn't have our best interests at heart?"

Staring at the older woman as she stared back with a small knowing smile on her face, Alinna caught movement to her left. She shifted her eyes just as she heard Dante's voice. He was talking with Tony T, James, and Gomez, saying something that caused all three guys to laugh.

"He is very handsome," Carmen said, also staring and watching Dante.

Not responding but catching Dante's eyes while he was still talking to Tony T and the others, Alinna sat watching him break away from all three guys and make his way over to where they were all sitting.

"What's up, ladies?" Dante said once he was within the group of women. He bent down and kissed Carmen's cheek, to which he received a smile as he squatted down beside the cushioned chair Carmen was sitting in. "I'm pretty sure I was the main topic of conversation since the three of you are upset with me right now. But I'm just trying to make sure everything is set up so Alinna can handle things with the Council. Carmen, I also want you to be Alinna's advisor until everything is in order, if that's alright with you?"

"That is perfectly fine, Dante. But I need you to understand something," Carmen expressed to him. "We understand what you're trying to do, but what's a concern to us are your plans that you refuse to share with us. We find out only when these plans begin unfolding."

Sighing as he looked from Carmen to Alinna to Natalie and back to Carmen, Dante sat down in the grass beside Carmen and said, "Truthfully, sometimes my plans come to me as I go. I just play them out as I make my moves. I really just move like I'm playing a chess game, making calculated moves. I understand I'm not playing only for myself, but for all of you. I gotta make the right moves because if I fuck up, I know I'm pulling each of you into danger, in addition to the family back in Miami. I'm playing for the checkmate."

Nodding her head in approval but also now seeing Dante in a new light after hearing the way he expressed himself, Carmen looked at her daughter and then over to Alinna. She noticed the same expression on both the women's faces, which showed her that both of them understood and forgave him.

* * *

Deep in thought as he stood under the wide shower head, Dante never heard the bathroom door open. But he did hear the shower door open. He turned around to see Natalie closing the door behind her.

"Hi, Papi!" Natalie said softly, walking under the shower spray and positioning herself in front of Dante, allowing the water to rain down over her chest.

Dante wrapped his arms around Natalie from the back and kissed her neck. He then asked, "What's on your mind, beautiful?"

"What makes you think something's on my mind?" she asked as she turned and faced Dante. "I could just want to shower with my husband."

"What's on your mind, Natalie?" Dante asked her again, pulling back away from her a little while, looking down into her eyes as she stood staring up at him.

Pulling Dante back up against her, only to wrap her arms around him and lay her head against his chest, Natalie stood there for a moment saying nothing. She finally began: "I understand what you're doing, Dante, and I support everything that's going on because I believe in anything you do. But what about me? You're making plans for everything for the family business, but you never said what you wanted me to do. Why?"

"First, because I don't want you in this part of the family business," Dante told her, then adding, "I'm always thinking about you, Natalie. You're going to be what we fall back on once we turn this business over to our kids. What is it that you like doing and that you can see yourself building into a business?"

"I love art, and I'm into decorating," she told Dante with a smile.

"What type of decorating?"

"Interior decorating," Natalie answered, still smiling. "Who do you think decorated this place we're living in? I gave instruction how I wanted it in here and what I wanted. I even did my mother and father's place myself."

"And what kind of art do you like?" Dante asked as his mind was already putting ideas together inside his head.

"Different types of art like paintings and old historical works," Natalie explained as she laid her head back against Dante's chest.

Quiet for a minute while thinking, Dante finally spoke, "I want you to get whatever license you need to open up and run an art museum and an interior decorating agency. We're going to invest however much it takes into both businesses, and you're going to be responsible. You think you can handle that, beautiful?"

Smiling even harder, excited about the news she was hearing, Natalie threw both her arms up and around Dante's neck, hugging him and then going up on her toes to kiss his lips.

"Ummm . . . excuse me, you two!" Alinna called out from outside the shower. "How long do you two plan on being in there? Emmy is done with the food and is waiting on the two of you!"

21

Dante woke up early the next day and left Alinna and Natalie asleep in bed. He then woke James so that the two of them could work out together.

Leaving the main house and walking over to the indoor gym, Gomez was already there working out. Dante nodded to the big man as James greeted the personal bodyguard with a touch of his fist.

"How long you been in here?" James asked as he walked over behind the weight bench where Dante was setting up to bench press.

"I've been at it maybe a little over twenty minutes," Gomez answered as he was curling a little over 120 pounds.

Assisting Dante with the weight he was basically lifting on his own, James stood watching and counting a set of twenty-five before Dante set down the bar.

"Gomez," Dante said after standing up so James could take his turn, "how long you been working for the Saldanas?"

"A little over ten years now."

"What is it you can tell me about the members in the Council Covenant?"

"Well, before I switched from being Dominic's bodyguard over to Natalie's, I used to sit in on the Council's meetings, and truthfully, it was always the same thing. Four middle-age guys fighting over the same thing: money, business, and locations. Nothing really got settled."

"Who were the ones who did most of the fighting?" Dante asked as he helped James set the bar back down.

Taking his turn next, running through another set of twenty-five, Dante set down the bar and got up, so James could go next.

"So who were the ones always fighting, Gomez?" Dante repeated again.

"Who was fighting?" Monica asked as she walked into the gym, drawing everyone's attention.

"Nobody's fighting, Monica," Dante told her but then turned back to Gomez, only to find the big man locked in, staring at Monica. "Gomez . . . come on, playboy! Focus with me. Who's the ones causing most of the fights in the Council meetings?"

Tearing his eyes away from the brown-skinned female in the thigh-length tights and matching sports bra, Gomez looked back at Dante and said, "Ummm . . . fights. It was either Dominic and some guy named Victor something, or Dominic and the guy I heard you talking with Mrs. Saldana about last night . . . Fredrick Roosevelt."

Nodding his head in thought, Dante focused on James, helping him put the weight bar back up. He then looked back toward Gomez and caught him staring at Monica and said, "Gomez, what about Samuel Atlas?"

"Who?" Gomez asked, looking back at Dante with a confused look in his eyes.

"Samuel Atlas," Dante repeated. "White guy with a long ponytail. Looks kind of like he's Italian."

"Naw . . . !" Gomez said, shaking his head. "I don't recognize the name. He must have come after the switch I went through to Natalie."

Nodding his head again, Dante sat down on the weight bench to take his turn, missing the way Monica was watching him.

* * *

The guys were finishing up in the gym when both Alinna and Natalie showed up and announced that Emmy had breakfast ready and was waiting on them. Dante took a quick shower and dressed in a Gucci suit with some brown Timbs and a padded brown leather jacket.

Dante made it to the breakfast table about the same time James was just sitting down. He then walked around to the head of the table, with Alinna on his right and Natalie on his left.

"Baby, I've got a meeting today with Samuel. You going with me?" Alinna asked Dante as they all sat eating breakfast.

"I've got something to handle today with Monica, but call me right after the meeting," Dante told her just as Monica walked into the room dressed in jeans, a tight-fitting black shirt, and a black leather jacket.

Dante shifted his eyes over at Gomez, who was once again staring at Monica as she sat down across from him at the table. Dante shook his head, only to look over at Natalie when she called his name, and said, "What's up, beautiful?"

"I'm meeting with both my mother and father. They want to talk about something, but mother wanted me to let you know she wants to see you for lunch."

"Where at?"

"The French Garden."

"Text me the location."

The family finished with conversation all around the table, except for Monica, who was the first to finish and first to leave the table. Dante then left the table with Alinna, pulling her to the side and saying, "This meeting you're having with this dude, Atlas. What's the meeting supposed to be about?"

"He wants to listen to some of the ideas and plans that you and I discussed, and even tell me some of the ideas he came up with," Alinna told Dante. "Why? What are you thinking?"

"I'm not sure yet," Dante answered. "It's something about homeboy. Do me a favor, though. Don't give up anything we've talked about. Give him some bullshit for now until I find out more about homeboy."

Starting to question Dante but thinking better about it, she just leaned in, kissed him, and said, "I'll call you right after the meeting."

Finding Monica outside walking up and down the drive, Dante loudly whispered, causing her to turn around and shout that she was on her cell phone. He nodded for her to follow him as he started toward the garage on the other side of the property.

"Where'd you get a cell phone from?" Dante asked once Monica caught up. Dante stood in front of a four-car garage and hit the remote given to him by Natalie to open the doors.

"It's a pre-paid, and I bought it at the airport when I got in," Monica answered him as she walked around the passenger side door of the Mercedes-Benz.

Dante unlocked the car doors, and they climbed in. He then started up the Benz and backed out of the garage.

"You not gonna ask who I was talking to?" Monica asked as they drove away from the mansion.

"Does it concern me?"

"Maybe!"

Slowly shifting his eyes over at Monica, he smirked at her. Dante focused back on the road but asked, "How's Agent Victor Murphy doing, Monica?"

Staring at Dante in shock and disbelief, she asked, "How the hell you know I was talking to Victor?"

"You just told me," Dante answered as he pulled out his phone, feeling it vibrating inside his pocket. He saw that it was Vanessa calling, so he asked, "What's up, Nessa!"

"Hi, Daddy."

Smiling at hearing Mya's voice, Dante said into the phone, "Hey, baby girl! When you learn how to use a cell phone?"

"It's easy, Daddy," Mya replied, giggling. "I miss you."

"I miss you, too, baby girl. Where's your brother?"

"He's with A.J. outside. You wanna talk to him?"

"Naw . . . Where's your Auntie Vanessa at?"

"She right here. Hold on, Daddy!"

Smiling while still waiting a few moments until Vanessa came on the phone, Dante said, "What's up, Vanessa?"

"What's up, big bruh? How's everything over there?"

"Just getting started, but look . . . I'm glad you let Mya call me . . ."

"I didn't let her," Vanessa told Dante interrupting him. "I didn't even know she had my phone or knew how to use one."

Shaking his head and smiling, Dante said, "Anyway . . . tell Dre I said to go ahead and release Monica's sister and brother-in-law but keep an eye on both of them."

"I'ma tell 'em . . . You need anything else?"

"Naw, but you need to go ahead and buy Mya and D.J. a cell phone. Gimme both their numbers and give 'em both mine and Alinna's."

"I'ma take care of that today. Let me call my sister, though, and see what Alinna's ass is up to."

"You better call now, because she got a meeting on some business later on."

"Alright, boy. I love you, Dante."

"I love you too, Vanessa," Dante told her, hanging up the phone. He then turned to Monica and asked, "You enjoy staring at me?"

"I'm just surprised to see you smiling," she told him. "You never smile."

"You just never seen me smile."

"So that was your daughter with Angela? Mya, right?"

Caught off guard, Dante looked over at Monica with a surprised expression on his face. He pulled the Benz over to the side of the road, ignoring the car horns from the other drivers behind him. He threw the Benz in park, swung around toward Monica, and inquired, "How the fuck you know about my fucking daughter?"

"Relax, dude!" Monica told him calmly, smiling a small grin. "You're not the only one that knows how to find out supposed secrets."

"Talk! Now Monica!"

"You don't scare me, Dante," Monica told him, still smiling, but then said, "I know all about you and Angela's deal and how she got pregnant from you. I even found out that she's out of the US now. But did you know she was the one that set you up?"

"What do you mean? How the fuck she set me up?"

"Who do you think told me about all the bodies you have, and even about the murder of Captain Ben Whitehead . . . which is why she made captain?"

Quiet as he sat staring out the car window after hearing what Monica had just told him, Dante then asked, "You telling me the truth, Monica?"

"I know your father was murdered and you don't know where your mother is, and that your father's friend raised you after he died. I know that Dre's mother was the one that took you in after your father's friend died . . ."

"Alright!" Dante said, cutting off Monica. He looked back over at her and said, "I believe you! But why are you telling me this now? Why put me in jail facing a life or death sentence that they were talking about?"

"Why do you think . . . you son of a bitch?" Monica said, suddenly angry now. "You killed my husband!"

Sighing deeply, Dante said, "What if I could prove that Alex was set up?"

"What the hell are you talking about?"

"Your husband was set up, and I can prove it."

"How?"

"Help me out here, and I'll prove it to you," Dante told her as he pulled back out into traffic.

"You still haven't told me how you plan on proving what you claim was a set-up on Alex," Monica told him, staring hard at Dante.

"I know where Angela is," Dante admitted, but then added, "Help me out here, and afterwards I'll take you with me to find Angela. Then you'll have your proof."

*   *   *

Finally reaching a luxury car dealership, only to end up fighting with Monica for five minutes about her wanting to leave and find a used car dealership, Dante just ignored her completely. He ended up selecting a Jaguar F-Type Coupe hardtop convertible.

Dante smirked, noticing that Monica didn't turn down the keys to the Jaguar when it was pulled around to the front of the dealership. He then said, "Change of heart about not wanting a brand new car?"

"I ain't no fool, Dante!" Monica told him with a smile as she walked over to the brand-new Jaguar.

"Let's find you some place to go shopping at," Dante said, walking toward his Benz.

Leaving the dealership and using his GPS inside the Benz, Dante found a surprisingly big mall with a huge parking lot.

After finding a place to park, Dante climbed from the Benz and saw Monica park two spaces down from him.

"I'm hungry," Monica told Dante as he walked up on her.

"You just ate breakfast."

"And I'm still hungry."

Shaking his head as he followed alongside her, walking through the parking lot, Dante found himself following her into the mall and in search of the food court.

*   *   *

Dante sat with Monica while she was eating two Big Macs from the McDonald's in the food court. He was drinking an orange soda, when his cell phone vibrated inside his pocket.

Pulling out his phone, Dante saw that he had a text message. He opened it and saw that it was from Natalie. It was the address to the restaurant he was supposed to meet Carmen at for lunch.

Once Monica finally finished eating, she and Dante both left the food court together. Monica had a satisfied smile on her face, which caused Dante to shake his head and smirk.

*   *   *

Two hours later and ten bags a piece, and still checking out more stores, Monica was ready to check out. Dante allowed her to shop, and even bought gifts for both Alinna and Natalie. Just as he was paying for a diamond-faced Movado watch, his phone started vibrating in his pocket again.

"You ready to go?" Monica asked, walking up beside Dante as he was pulling out his cell phone.

"You finished?" Dante asked, seeing Natalie's number on the screen.

"I'm ready," Monica told him, waving for Dante to leave the store with her.

"What's up, beautiful?" Dante said, but then he immediately stopped in his tracks when he heard crying and yelling in the background over his phone. "Natalie! Natalie! What's up? What's going on?"

"Dante! Dante! It's Daddy!" Natalie got out, before she started crying hysterically.

"Natalie . . . talk to me!" Dante yelled, already running toward the exit. "Baby, what's going on? Talk to me!"

"Dante, what's going on?" Monica asked, running and trying to keep up with a surprisingly fast Dante.

"I don't know! Natalie was . . ."

"Dante, this Tony T!" Dante heard.

Stopping in the middle of what he was telling Monica, he said into the phone just as he and Monica shot out the exit door of the mall, "Bruh, what the fuck going on?"

"Dante, man! It's Dominic. He was set up!"

"Fuck do you mean set up?"

"He was meeting somebody for some business meeting, and once we got there, all we met was a bunch of niggas with guns."

"Shit!" Dante said as he and Monica stopped at her Jaguar. "What about Dominic?"

"Bruh, he got hit twice. It ain't looking good," Tony T explained. "We ain't sure what's going on right now. The doctor's got him."

"Where the fuck ya'll at?" Dante asked, completely pissed off.

"We at Phoenix Memorial."

Hanging up the phone, Dante handed Monica the rest of the bags he was holding as she asked, "What's it about?"

"Natalie's father was shot. He's at Phoenix Memorial, and they not sure if he'll live," Dante explained. He then pulled out his left-side Glock from its holster and handed it to Monica. "You gonna need one. Shit about to get real stupid in Phoenix!"

To be continued . . .

BOOKS BY GOOD2GO AUTHORS

GOOD 2 GO FILMS PRESENTS

THE HAND I WAS DEALT- FREE WEB SERIES
NOW AVAILABLE ON YOUTUBE!
YOUTUBE.COM/SILKWHITE212

SEASON TWO NOW AVAILABLE

To order books, please fill out the order form below:

To order films please go to ***www.good2gofilms.com***

Name:_____

Address:_____

City: _____ State: _____ Zip Code: _____

Phone:_____

Email:_____

Method of Payment: Check   VISA   MASTERCARD

Credit Card#:_____

Name as it appears on card: _____

Signature: _____

Item Name	Price	Qty	Amount
48 Hours to Die – Silk White	$14.99		
Business Is Business – Silk White	$14.99		
Business Is Business 2 – Silk White	$14.99		
Business Is Business 3 – Silk White	$14.99		
Childhood Sweethearts – Jacob Spears	$14.99		
Childhood Sweethearts 2 – Jacob Spears	$14.99		
Childhood Sweethearts 3 - Jacob Spears	$14.99		
Flipping Numbers – Ernest Morris	$14.99		
Flipping Numbers 2 – Ernest Morris	$14.99		
He Loves Me, He Loves You Not - Mychea	$14.99		
He Loves Me, He Loves You Not 2 - Mychea	$14.99		
He Loves Me, He Loves You Not 3 - Mychea	$14.99		
He Loves Me, He Loves You Not 4 – Mychea	$14.99		
He Loves Me, He Loves You Not 5 – Mychea	$14.99		
Lost and Turned Out – Ernest Morris	$14.99		
Married To Da Streets – Silk White	$14.99		
M.E.R.C. - Make Every Rep Count Health and Fitness	$14.99		
My Besties – Asia Hill	$14.99		
My Besties 2 – Asia Hill	$14.99		
My Besties 3 – Asia Hill	$14.99		
My Besties 4 – Asia Hill	$14.99		
My Boyfriend's Wife - Mychea	$14.99		
My Boyfriend's Wife 2 – Mychea	$14.99		
Never Be The Same – Silk White	$14.99		
Stranded – Silk White	$14.99		
Slumped – Jason Brent	$14.99		
Tears of a Hustler - Silk White	$14.99		
Tears of a Hustler 2 - Silk White	$14.99		
Tears of a Hustler 3 - Silk White	$14.99		
Tears of a Hustler 4- Silk White	$14.99		
Tears of a Hustler 5 – Silk White	$14.99		
Tears of a Hustler 6 – Silk White	$14.99		

The Panty Ripper - Reality Way	$14.99		
The Panty Ripper 3 – Reality Way	$14.99		
The Teflon Queen – Silk White	$14.99		
The Teflon Queen 2 – Silk White	$14.99		
The Teflon Queen 3 – Silk White	$14.99		
The Teflon Queen 4 – Silk White	$14.99		
The Teflon Queen 5 – Silk White	$14.99		
The Teflon Queen 6 - Silk White	$14.99		
The Vacation – Silk White	$14.99		
Tied To A Boss - J.L. Rose	$14.99		
Tied To A Boss 2 - J.L. Rose	$14.99		
Time Is Money - Silk White	$14.99		
Young Goonz – Reality Way	$14.99		
Subtotal:			
Tax:			
Shipping (Free) U.S. Media Mail:			
Total:			

Make Checks Payable To:
Good2Go Publishing
7311 W Glass Lane,
Laveen, AZ 85339

CPSIA information can be obtained
at www.ICGtesting.com
Printed in the USA
LVOW04s1440111116
512626LV00007B/422/P